D

A Candlelight Ecstasy Romance®

4

"I WANT YOU AS MY LOVER," QUINN MURMURED.

Sydney's green eyes flashed. "Why, you split-tongued devil! You promised me we'd be just friends! I'm not ready to get involved!"

"Don't take it so seriously, Syd," Quinn drawled. "Being lovers doesn't mean we have to get involved. After all, I want my freedom. But I could be a good man to have around—"

"And whenever you wanted someone to warm your bed, you'd give me a call, is that it?" she whispered. "Sounds simple enough. Only trouble is, I don't go to bed with a man that easily."

Quinn's eyes caressed her face. "Well, maybe I can change your mind."

Be sure to read this month's
CANDLELIGHT ECSTASY CLASSIC ROMANCES . . .

THE TAWNY GOLD MAN, *Amii Lorin*
GENTLE PIRATE, *Jayne Castle*

CANDLELIGHT ECSTASY ROMANCES®

SWEET REVENGE

Tate McKenna

A CANDLELIGHT ECSTASY ROMANCE®

Published by
Dell Publishing Co., Inc.
1 Dag Hammarskjold Plaza
New York, New York 10017

Dell ® TM 681510, Dell Publishing Co., Inc.

Candlelight Ecstasy Romance®, 1,203,540, is a registered trademark of Dell Publishing Co., Inc., New York, New York.

ISBN: 0-440-18431-2

Printed in the United States of America

August 1986

10 9 8 7 6 5 4 3 2 1

WFH

To Our Readers:

We have been delighted with your enthusiastic response to Candlelight Ecstasy Romances®, and we thank you for the interest you have shown in this exciting series.

In the upcoming months we will continue to present the distinctive sensuous love stories you have come to expect only from Ecstasy. We look forward to bringing you many more books from your favorite authors and also the very finest work from new authors of contemporary romantic fiction.

As always, we are striving to present the unique, absorbing love stories that you enjoy most—books that are more than ordinary romance. Your suggestions and comments are always welcome. Please write to us at the address below.

Sincerely,

The Editors
Candlelight Romances
1 Dag Hammarskjold Plaza
New York, New York 10017

SWEET REVENGE

PROLOGUE

Sydney would never forget the day her husband left. Left? That was too nice a word for what he did. *Desertion* was what the Family Aid counselor called it. *Devastation* was what it created in her life. And the pain was deep and lasting.

Sometimes when she closed her eyes at night, Sydney could still see that note lying on the kitchen table, just a simple scrap of paper with a few words scrawled across the surface. But that simple note had changed her life. Eight years of marriage, reduced to a couple of brief, unemotional words.

Even now, the memory brought a certain panic, a fear of the unknown, an insecurity, to her heart. She was all alone. Just her and Chad. They would have to make it—or not—on their own.

It had rained that day. Rained all day and night. The constant drizzle had fueled her own tears and increased her worry that something had happened to him. It had taken him two days to call her. Two days of distraught emotions, arguments with the police, who refused to become involved in a family matter. Two days of phoning everyone she knew trying to find him.

Then came the phone call. The call she'd waited for so frantically. She was shaky, nervous, wildly ecstatic, angry—every emotion at once—when she recognized his voice and realized he was safe. Not dead.

"I'm not coming back, Sydney."

"What? Why? What's wrong with you, Daniel?"

"It's over. I'll send you some money. Don't try to find me. We're through. I can't help it. Neither can you."

That night, Sydney finished a whole bottle of cheap wine. The next day, as she gulped numerous cups of black coffee, she regretted every sweet sip. But her regret and self-pity soon turned to bitterness. And the bitterness eventually evolved into a tough determination.

Daniel sent money, all right. But it was too little, too late. She lost the house and had to move into an apartment. By then, the biggest regret was that they had to give Chad's dog away. A four-year-old couldn't be expected to understand why they couldn't keep the rangy Labrador in the apartment complex. And Sydney had to take the blame. After all, she was moving them, wasn't she? God, she hated Daniel for doing that to her. To Chad.

Determination kept her going. She worked part-time, finishing college, taking money from Daniel when he offered it. But she hated every moment of the dependency.

Deep in her heart, Sydney vowed revenge. She was determined to become financially independent. The words had an admirable ring. That was her goal. To be able to make it on her own and do it well. *To show Daniel that she could make it without him and in spite of his desertion.* That would be her sweetest revenge.

CHAPTER ONE

"How does that feel?"

Sydney readjusted her hips. "Perfect, absolutely perfect!"

"Now, loosen your hands. They're too tight. Hold it lightly. Caress it."

She complied. "Like this?"

He nodded tersely. "Yes, yes, that's it. A little higher."

She readjusted her hands. "How's this?"

"Better. Now, relax your back and shoulders. You're too stiff."

"How can I relax when I have so many things to think about?" she murmured glumly. "This hand like this. That hand like that. Fingers interwoven, loosely. Left foot here. Right foot there. Hips even. Butt tucked. Shoulders straight. Elbows in. Head down. And relax!"

"You've got it!"

"I can't breathe."

"Breathe slow and easy, steady."

"Yeah, but can I hit a golf ball this way?" Sydney complained and brought the golf club back with perfect form. A slow smile spread across her face as she

15

appreciated the weight and feel of the new club. "Oh, yes, how sweet it is." She followed through with a motion credible for a novice.

At precisely that moment, the club head accidentally came into contact with a stray golf ball lying on the small square of Astroturf green.

The white ball shot across the sports equipment store with remarkable speed and accuracy. She stared in amazement—and young Randy, the clerk, stared in horror—as the ball skimmed head-high through the leotard rack, past the barbells, over the row of football helmets, and bounced against the wall next to the display rack of fishing rods.

The erring ball barely missed the head of a customer browsing through the fishing equipment. His foul expletive could be heard resoundingly throughout the store. Fortunately, it was an off hour and there were no other customers in the place.

"Oh dear, I didn't mean to—" Sydney gasped, unable to move.

Randy tore across the store to check on his customer. "Are—are you all right, mister? It—it was an accident, sir."

"An accident!" The voice boomed, echoing off the wall of surfboards at the far end of the store. "Damnation! It's dangerous in here. An innocent bystander could get killed in this place, kid!"

Sydney finally made her way through the obstacle course of sports equipment. "Don't blame Randy. It was an accident and my fault. I'm sorry. I didn't hit you, did I?"

The irate customer turned intense blue eyes on Sydney. "So this was your fault?" He stared, waiting for her full confession. His eyes were the bluest she'd ever seen, admittedly angry, but with a touch of something else—maybe humor?

She smiled, hoping to soften his glare. "Yes, it was me. Honestly, I didn't see that ball. I certainly didn't mean to hit it. And not toward you."

Judging by his expression, he didn't find her explanation amusing. "Damn it, lady! Don't you look when you swing a club? You're deadly with that thing! How in hell could you miss seeing a golf ball? That's why they're white. So you can see 'em. What do you need? Red polka dots?"

"The ball wasn't supposed to be there," she explained rationally. "That's a practice putting green."

"Then why in God's name did you tee off and bang that misguided missile like a bat outta hell?"

"Well I—I told you, I didn't see the ball. It—wasn't directly on the tee. It was just lying there."

"Waiting for your club to swing around and find it? You must be a walking hazard on the golf course. Ever played golf with Jerry Ford?" He tilted his head of curly brown hair questioningly.

Sydney glared at him. This stubborn man wasn't about to give an inch. Her emerald eyes flashed with growing agitation. "I said I'm sorry. What more do you want? Did the ball actually hit you?"

"I wouldn't be standing here if it had," he answered gruffly. "I'd be stretched out on the floor, waiting for an ambulance!"

Sydney considered briefly that he just *might* yet be stretched out on the floor if he continued his belligerence. "Oh, I didn't hit the ball that hard." She shifted the golf club to her other hand, resisting the notion to bean him with it.

"Hard? Hell, you don't have to hit a golf ball hard to do damage to a human skull."

"Well, maybe the average human skull, but yours seems to be hard enough to withstand anything, including a reasonable apology!"

"Uh, Mrs. Jacques—" Randy interrupted miserably.

She looked into the stricken face of the clerk, who was watching their verbal volley helplessly. What was wrong with her, anyway? "Sorry, Randy. I don't know what got into me. Go ahead and wait on your customer, and I'll just go practice my swing. Please, take care of him first."

Randy gave her a grateful smile. "Thanks, Mrs. Jacques." He turned to the customer. "Now, can I help you, sir?"

Sydney tucked the shaft of the golf club under her arm, clamped her teeth together, and started back across the store.

"Uh, lady?" It was the curly-haired customer again. "Do me a favor. Don't mess around with any more balls, okay? At least, not until I get out of the store."

Suddenly, Sydney blushed. The look in the man's eyes was definitely suggestive—more than humorous, downright bawdy! Damn him, anyway. "Don't worry. No more b—alls." She finished the word weakly.

Turning away quickly from those daring blue eyes, Sydney melted into the background, wishing for all the world that she could crawl into the tiny cup that served as the hole for the practice putting green. Whatever made her repeat such an inane, suggestive remark to an absolute stranger? Hadn't she learned anything about keeping from getting flustered in that interviewing class at school? Well, this man had certainly sent her spinning, and she resented him for it. Maybe it was his eyes that had such an effect on her.

Sydney was unaware of the engaging gaze of those daring blue eyes as the customer watched her slink away. There was definite humor in their azure depths —also flagrant masculine admiration.

She had a nice enough body, he thought. Straight back, slender waist, rather skimpy hips, all tucked neatly into a simple white T-shirt and black shorts. But those legs! They seemed to go on forever! Long and shapely and straight as an arrow. Her thighs were firm and met snugly along the inside all the way to her knees, making him want to run his hand along that sensuous stretch. And the flat, tender area behind her knees was made to be touched!

"Did you want to try on these waders, sir?"

The man turned back to Randy, brushing aside his thoughts. "Yes. My boot size is eleven."

Without looking toward her nemesis, Sydney gave a few halfhearted swings with the new club, then put it back in the rack. By the time Randy had left his customer and approached her again, she was browsing through a stack of visors that had TALLAHASSEE spelled across the brim. "I can't interest you in that new club today, Mrs. Jacques?"

"No, Randy. I was only looking, anyway. It doesn't seem to be a very lucky club for me."

"It's a good, solid club, Mrs. Jacques. Have you taken up golf?"

She laughed wryly. "When would I ever play? Between midnight and six? You know I can't afford such an expensive hobby, Randy. I stopped by because Lora said you might be able to help me with a class at school."

Randy looked surprised. "Mom said that? What could I do?"

Sydney smiled. Lora was her closest friend, and her son, Randy, would soon be graduating from high school. "Since you work here at the Sports Center, we figured you knew what was happening in town in the sports scene. Like the Ladies Professional Golfing Association that's coming to town. And which people are involved in sports."

"Yeah, I guess I know that much." He shrugged. "The LPGA is still several weeks away, though."

"Randy," Sydney pursued thoughtfully, "do you know if any of the golfing celebrities have come to town early to practice for the tournament?"

Randy gave her a doubtful look.

"You see, I need an interesting character, preferably a celebrity, to tape for the final exam in my interviewing class at the university," Sydney explained. "Can you think of anyone here in town who's a national sports figure? Gee, I wish the tournament weren't three weeks away. Wouldn't I just love to interview someone like JoAnne Carner or Nancy Lopez! That would blow my teacher away and cinch an A in the course!"

Randy scratched his head and let his eyes wander around the store. "I can't think of any. How about one of the golf pros at the country club?"

Sydney made a bored face. "Dull. But I might have to go that route. What I *really* need is someone big to impress this teacher. Somebody with national ac-claim."

"What about him?" Randy aimed his thumb over his shoulder.

"Who?" Her eyes traveled in the general direction of his thumb and rested on the curly brown head of the irate customer she'd almost beaned. He was stand-ing with his back to them, his shoulders broad and the rest of his body stuffed into shapeless, camouflage hip waders that extended loosely above his waist.

"The man you nearly hit with the golf ball." Randy hid a youthful smile. "He used to be a big pro golfer. Sometimes I see his picture in magazine ads and things like that. He'd be a national character for you."

She shook her head immediately. "I don't think so. An ex-golfing pro? What does he do now?"

"Nothing, I guess. Doesn't have to. This guy was on top for many years, made lots of money. Oh, excuse me, Mrs. Jacques. I think I'd better help him with those waders he's trying on." Randy hurried back to the fishing department.

"Yes, please. Keep him happy," Sydney mumbled, unconsciously reconsidering the ex-pro golfer as a prospect. Big name, huh? Well, it was worth a try. He was better than nothing for this final interview.

Sydney ambled toward the fishing department, stop-ping along the way to admire the barbell system, until the customer had finished his shopping. She had done enough damage already. She certainly didn't want to anger him more and interfere with Randy's sales. Judging by the size of the pile of equipment he'd accu-mulated, it would be a good one.

"That's about it." He nodded to the rubber waders. "Ring them up along with the rest."

"Yes, sir!" Randy hurried to the cash register, his arms loaded with fishing paraphernalia. With a sale like this, he could handle an occasional hassle between customers.

Sydney felt some relief from the guilt she was carrying because of the scene she'd caused with the customer. She would have felt extremely guilty if the man had just walked out, and for a minute that's what she'd feared he would do.

"Looking for a lost ball, lady?"

She jerked her head up, startled, and blushed at his words. "Uh, no. I—I wanted to talk to you for a minute."

He folded his arms. "So talk. You don't mind if I keep my distance?"

"First, let me apologize again for the incident with the golf ball earlier."

"You mean when you nearly killed me with your wild stroke? Consider it forgotten."

Honestly! For two cents she'd walk out herself! But Sydney needed him for that class interview. "Thank you for being so charitable," she muttered dryly, then remembered her mission and forced a smile. "Randy tells me you're a, uh, retired golfer."

"Retired? I don't think we golfers ever retire," he chuckled, and she figured it was a joke only golfers would appreciate.

"Well, I mean, retired from the professional circuit," she amended judiciously. Is this how the interview would go? The old "tooth extraction technique," as her professor would say. *Smile while you're slowly, but surely, pulling those answers out.* This man might be her first challenge for that newly learned interviewing skill.

"Okay, I'll buy that." He nodded approvingly. "Retired from the circuit. But I still consider myself a professional golfer. Sometimes I teach or give special workshops or do other things I enjoy."

"Do you really enjoy it now that the challenge is gone?" She tossed the gauntlet back to him.

"What makes you think the challenge is gone?" His blue eyes caught hers. They were beautiful, humorous, sexy eyes, and Sydney tried to avoid their barely disguised innuendoes while meeting his gaze. It wasn't easy.

"Isn't it?"

"Of course not. I'm doing other things now. Different things. If I didn't like them, I wouldn't do them. I'm past the era in my life when I do what's expected. Now I just do what I want to do."

"How lucky you are," she observed wryly, trying to keep her own personal opinions well-hidden. That was important for an interviewer. "Would you be willing to talk about your, uh, new life-style in an interview?"

He shifted and looked at her anew. "I might be willing to talk about the upcoming tournament. Which media?"

She almost hated to tell him and mumbled the words, "My interviewing class at the university." It sounded so schoolgirlish.

"Your what?" His blue eyes opened wider, as if he hadn't heard her correctly.

She rushed to explain, hoping she could jazz it up a bit. He would be doing her a favor, but why in the world would he want to do that, especially after she'd nearly knocked him out with a golf ball? She would have to come up with a good, solid reason.

Taking a deep breath, she decided the truth would have to do. "Frankly, it's for my final exam in an interviewing class. We have to interview an interesting character on videotape. The teacher evaluates it and grades us on our techniques. Later, the class views the tapes so we'll all benefit from each other's interviews. I'm interested in sports reporting, so naturally I'd prefer to feature a well-known sports figure. Someone like yourself." She smiled encouragingly.

"So the only people who'll see this little interview are thirty or so students in your class?"

Her heart sank. He looked unenthusiastic. Why should he do her this favor if all he got out of it was an audience of thirty? She had to offer more.

"What if—what if I could get you a local TV spot for an interview where you could talk about the Golf Charity or anything you wanted to? Would you do it for me then?" Sydney realized she was going out on a limb, but she'd worry about that later.

His interest perked appreciably. "Could you get me a spot? In that case, I'd love to do it. We could use some publicity for the tournament."

She smiled hopefully. "I work part-time at WTAL-TV, and I have a few connections." *Very few!* she thought. "I'll see what I can do for you. When would be a good time for us to do the interview?"

"Make it soon. I'm getting ready to head out of town for a fishing trip. How about tomorrow?"

"Tomorrow's fine." She nodded, already wondering what she'd ask an ex-pro golfer in an interview. She

24

didn't have long to figure it out. "I work in the morning. How about the afternoon? Around four?"

"Okay."

"Could you meet me at the Fine Arts Building on campus? We'll do the taping there."

"You got it. See you then." He smiled pleasantly, for the first time since their encounter.

"Oh, uh, what's your—I'm Sydney Jacques."

"Well-known, huh?" He grinned devilishly. In their entire exchange, they hadn't introduced themselves. And obviously she didn't know his name. He extended a hand. "I'm Quinn Robinson. Nice to meet you, Sydney."

She shook his hand, rather limply she was afraid, for his grip was firm and warm. And strong. And he continued to cradle her hand in his. "Quinn. Nice to meet you, too. And thanks for this interview. I—I hope you won't be sorry."

"Let's hope not." He smiled. "See you tomorrow. And please don't bring your golf club. We wouldn't want another near-disaster."

"Nor your childishness preserved on tape!" She fumed inside, realizing he wasn't about to let her forget the incident. At this point, she didn't care if he canceled the interview. As likely as not, he'd mention their little episode right in the middle of the taping, and *that* she definitely did not want! It certainly wouldn't bring her an A. And that's all she wanted from this golfer. He was a means to an end, that was all.

"Just keep the questions on golf, and we'll do fine," he instructed, finally releasing her hand.

Sydney felt as though her hand and her entire body

had been wrung out. The man did strange things to her. Either she was saying something absolutely inane, or she was railing at him like a banshee. The interview would be one time when a written script would be in order. "We'll stick to the subject, I promise. And Quinn, I want this interview to be very professional. This is no free ride. It isn't merely for a grade—it could mean a future job." *A better job.* "It means a lot to me."

He assessed the sudden seriousness in her green eyes. "I can be as professional as you, Sydney."

"No innuendoes?"

He grinned, slowly, devilishly. "Can't you handle them?"

She stiffened. "I'd rather not have to, especially on this tape. It's like a class exam, remember?" Could she trust him? Suddenly, she felt she was in over her head with this man. What if he ruined the interview and her chances at a good grade and the job!

Abruptly, he reached toward her, feathering her sensitive cheekbone with a single finger. "Don't worry. I won't say anything to bring too much pink right here."

Sydney hid a gasp at the gentleness of his touch. Even his voice had softened, and he was no longer the bastion of churlishness.

It had been so long since a man had touched her like that, gently, and made her feel like a woman. Daniel had never cared to caress her unless he wanted sex in return. She'd forgotten what gentleness was like. Touching without demands. It was oh, so nice. . . . She goaded herself back to reality.

"Thank you, Quinn. I'll rely on your professionalism," she managed to say. He nodded silently before turning away. His discerning blue eyes had whipped her into an inner froth, and she felt relief that he was leaving.

Weakly, Sydney watched from behind the rack of baseball gloves as Quinn paid for the goods Randy had stacked by the register. She tried not to notice the ease with which he lifted the huge box and carted it out to his glossy black and red pickup truck. Now that he was out of those bulky waders, she could see how wonderful he really looked. His shoulders were broad and his arms were muscular and tanned, probably from years of swinging a golf club.

His brown plaid shirt was tucked into the trim waist of tan slacks, bringing her attention to his slim male hips. Although he was dressed very casually, there was an air of affluence about Quinn Robinson.

A big name in golf, Randy had said. A wealthy man who did what he wanted. She sighed at the preposterous thought. Who could do that these days? Regardless, she knew he would make an interesting interview, and she had Randy to thank for suggesting him.

When Quinn pulled away in his shiny new Ford pickup, Sydney ambled nonchalantly out of hiding. Digging into her purse for her car keys, she asked, "Randy, where can I get some information on professional golfers? And fast!"

As she drove through town, Sydney thought about Quinn Robinson and what in the world she would ask him in the interview tomorrow. Glancing at the stack of magazines beside her, she knew she had some heavy studying to do this evening. And a dreadful project it promised to be, too. *Golfer's Digest* and *Golf Master* were not her idea of titillating reading but, given her complete ignorance of the field, Sydney had to prepare. After all, this was exactly what any good reporter had to do.

She smiled with a spark of hope. Maybe this interview with Quinn Robinson would help her work her way out of her internship job at the station and into something professional. *Like sportscaster.*

Thoughts of her job reminded Sydney of the brash promise she'd made to Quinn about getting him a spot on TV. She wasn't exactly in a position where the station manager asked for her input. They called her a communications assistant, which sounded pretty good on the surface. Actually, she was everyone's assistant. It was a gofer job. But she was learning a lot about the industry. At least, that's what she kept telling herself.

All that would change when she got her degree in communications. Three more weeks. Then nothing would stop her! She could tell Daniel to take a flying leap!

Sydney pulled the car to a stop, and the pending interview with the handsome Quinn Robinson, her upcoming graduation, her job, even her problems with Daniel fled her mind.

Sydney opened the car door and her arms to the small boy who hopped awkwardly toward her. Her heart pounded with love and delight, and she accepted his choking hug eagerly. No matter what happened and no matter how difficult things were, she would always be grateful to Daniel for giving her Chad.

She had been through hell for this child, and she

28

was prepared to do whatever was necessary to keep him. They would make it. Together.

"Hi, Mommy! Guess what we did in school. We pretended to be our favorite animals. I'm a frog today!" Chad grinned up at her, and she recognized her own bright smile and Daniel's blue eyes. He was a handsome mixture of both of them.

"You make a nice frog." She smiled. "Well, hop in the car so we can get home."

"Okay, Mama Frog." He giggled and scrambled into the front seat. "Can I have a snack when we get home, Mom?"

"You hungry, darling?" Sydney buckled him into the seat.

"Um-hum! Real hungry! I need a doughnut!"

"I'll fix you a pot pie the minute we get home. How does that sound?"

"Not as good as a doughnut," he confessed. "If I eat all the carrots and peas 'n everything yucky, then can I have a doughnut?"

She laughed and pulled the car out into the traffic. "We'll see, Chad."

He strained his short frame to look out the passenger window. "Is Daddy coming for me this weekend?"

Sydney caught her breath. When would she get used to their new life-style, this every-other-weekend method of parenting? Naturally, Chad looked forward to time with his father. "Not this weekend, Chad." Half the time, Daniel didn't even show up, disappointing Chad even more.

"Why did Daddy have to find a new home?" His blue eyes dug fiercely into her.

Somehow, Sydney couldn't bring herself to tell a

five-year-old the truth. How could she say his father was living with another woman? That wasn't a new home—it was a new bed. The situation was hard enough for her to accept. Chad would have to wait until he was older. "You'll have to ask him yourself, darling."

"Are we going to find another new home?"

"No, we're going to stay right where we are."

"Aw, shucks."

"You want to move again?" She gave him a curious glance. "We just got settled in the apartment."

"No, I want Mrs. Frye to move," Chad answered readily. "She's always telling me to 'be-e-e-e quiet' and 'walk slowly in the halls, young man.' "

Sydney stopped for a traffic light and grasped his little hand. "Tell you what, Chad. We'll go to the park Saturday, and you can run and make all the noise you want. Maybe we'll fly some kites or something."

"Yeah! You're fun, Mom. I'll bet I can fly mine the highest!"

The traffic light changed, and Sydney's foot dropped to the accelerator. "Probably." Already, her thoughts were on her immediate objective: an interview with an ex-professional golfer and his riveting blue eyes.

CHAPTER TWO

When Sydney curled up that night with her resources, she uncovered the history of the remarkable, dynamic Quinn Robinson. And she was impressed.

One magazine told of young Quinn Robinson winning a golf scholarship to Florida State University. Another told of the college student-turned-professional in his sophomore year. There were scores of how-to articles by Quinn Robinson, winner of numerous championships spanning a thirteen-year career. Then a shoulder injury, repeated surgery, the ultimatum. QUINN ROBINSON RETIRES FROM GOLF AT THE PEAK OF HIS CAREER.

Sydney became caught up in the disappointment he must have felt. What now? Why, just like many professional athletes, he'd turned to advertising.

His ads weren't limited to golfing equipment, but included his many hobbies, like fishing. One ad stood out in particular. In the ad, Quinn perched in a boat on a gorgeous lake ringed by mountains, holding a sleek, black fishing rod and sporting a sassy grin. Beneath the nature scene was the bold slogan, WIMPY RODS CATCH WIMPY FISH. The phrase was also emblazoned on his sweat shirt. Obviously, neither the man nor his choice of fishing rods was wimpy.

At midnight, Sydney folded away her copious notes and well-thumbed magazines. Tonight she had entered a world she never realized existed, a world where play was taken very seriously. She now had a pretty good idea about the golfer's vocabulary and equipment, his successes and disappointments. That should carry her into the interview tomorrow. The rest depended on her rapport with Quinn Robinson.

She flipped off the bedside lamp and settled against her pillow in the darkness. Most disturbing to Sydney, though, was the realization that a definitive picture of Quinn was emerging. And she couldn't dismiss him.

Quinn. She repeated his name silently, letting it roll around her head. It even sounded strong and sure, very much like the man she'd met today. Was it only today? Strangely, she felt that she had known him longer. Sydney fell asleep with thoughts of Quinn Robinson still in her head.

Sydney paced in front of the Fine Arts Building and checked her watch again. He was fifteen minutes late. She had reserved that taping room for a specific time. What if they missed it altogether? And Quinn was going out of town tomorrow. Where was he, anyway? Surely he wouldn't stand her up!

Her anticipation over the interview was enhanced by the fact that she just plain wanted to see Quinn again. Last night, as she had studied the trail of the professional golfer, the man named Quinn Robinson became her focus. Her distraction. She couldn't deny wanting to be with him again, to experience the distraction, the fun, the unique interplay between man and woman. She remembered Quinn's gentle touch on her cheek and longed again for . . .

"Sorry I'm late, but I lost track of the time. Packing for the big fishing trip tomorrow."

With a startled blink, Sydney gazed into the smiling blue eyes of Quinn Robinson. He was slightly breathless, and it gave him an appealing, sensuous look. Apparently, he had just jogged across the campus. His hair, a riot of walnut brown curls, framed his tanned face. He exuded a masculine aura that made her suddenly want to reach out, take his gentle hand, and run away.

Dangerous thoughts for a woman who was about to risk her future on an interview with a man who was virtually a stranger!

She muffled an impulsive, *That's all right. At least, you're here!* Instead, she jibed, "We may not have time for the interview. The room's reserved, you know."

"Then what are we waiting for?" He took her elbow easily and hurried her into the building.

Sydney paused before they started up the first flight of stairs and swallowed her pride along with her anger. After all, he was doing her a tremendous favor. "Quinn, thank you for coming today. I realize you didn't have to do this."

He looked at her seriously. "Did you think I wouldn't?"

"When you were late, I thought you might have changed your mind."

"I'm a man of my word, Sydney." His eyes reaffirmed his statement as he nodded toward the stairs.

Quinn followed her, half a step behind, watching

her smooth, feminine motion. She looked completely different today in her silk suit and tailored blouse with beige and cranberry stripes, embellished with two simple but elegant strands of gold chain. Her auburn hair framed her face, and when the light hit it just right, tawny gold highlights were visible.

Closer inspection revealed tiny pearl teardrops in each pierced earlobe. Something about this woman compelled him more than any he'd seen in years. It was more than mere physical attraction, although she was a damned good-looking woman. There was something irresistible about her that drew him to her. No, he couldn't have stood her up today. He wanted to see her again.

Sydney fidgeted with her notes and babbled about the weather as they hustled up the three flights of stairs to the taping room. At the top, she halted to catch her breath. "And I'm glad you wore something decent, Quinn. I pictured you in those awful camouflage things you bought at the sports center yesterday."

"Waders?" he asked with a laugh. "I wouldn't do that to you. After your comment, I figured you wanted this interview to look and sound as professional as possible. So I dressed up for you. I didn't wear a tie because I don't own one."

"You look fine." Sydney decided he looked wonderful in a freewheeling, casual way. His rust-tone linen sport coat contrasted with the tab-collared ecru cotton shirt and snug-fitting tan slacks. She grinned good-naturedly. "Actually, I had a greater fear that you'd appear in that awful sweat shirt you wore in the wimpy fish ad."

Quinn threw his head back in a hearty laugh. "You've been doing your homework, I see."

"Of course I have. That's part of a reporter's job. And I'll admit I learned a different language that I never knew existed. Golfing is a whole new world."

"What do you think about my previous life?"

"Interesting."

"A noncommittal answer, if I ever heard one."

She looked anxiously down the hall. "If you've caught your breath, I think we'd better go on in."

"You're nervous about this, aren't you, Sydney?"

"A little."

"Don't worry. It'll be fine."

"Easy for you to say." She bristled slightly at his offhand attitude. "Obviously this little interview means nothing to you, Quinn, but everything hinges on it for me."

"Then we'll make it a good one." He took her hand and squeezed it reassuringly. "I've done hundreds of these. I'll help you through." His thumb scraped over her fingers and his stomach knotted immediately. He quelled the urge to lift those fingers to his lips and press a kiss along each knuckle. Even though they were soft and cool to the touch, they set him on fire.

"Thanks," she mumbled, trying to tug her hand loose casually.

He held it for a second longer, then released her. "I won't clam up on you. I'm a good talker."

"I can see you are." She swallowed hard. And good at other things that are so important, like a gentle touch at just the right time.

"No innuendoes, I promise." He grinned.

They entered the taping room laughing, and some of

35

Sydney's apprehension disappeared. Strangely, she felt confident that Quinn would help her through this.

With a signal to the cameraman, Sydney took a deep breath and introduced Quinn to the make-believe audience.

"Quinn Robinson is a man who knows what he's doing. In addition to being a professional golfer, he teaches golfing workshops, has a best-selling golfing video, fishes in remote trout streams around the world, trains bird dogs, and endorses various sports equipment in magazine ads. He is a man who takes his playing seriously."

Quinn raised his eyebrows. She'd done her homework, all right. In fact, it must have taken some extensive research to uncover such detailed information about him. What else did she know? That his games had ruined his marriage? That he still struggled with the guilt?

Sydney's questions began innocently enough with the typical "How did you get started?" but her confidence grew as the interview proceeded. Quinn was a relaxed talker, and Sydney didn't have to struggle to extract answers. She led him into telling about his video and the importance of casting action to the serious fisherman.

Amazingly, he was serious. Sydney's attitude was more tongue in cheek. She tactically steered him away from a promising fish tale with a smooth "We'll catch your story about the one that got away another time, Quinn."

His eyes flickered again, this time with admiration for her skill. She was good, all right. But he'd been easy on her, too. Just given her straight answers.

Sydney felt her pulse rise. The end was near, and all had gone well. One last comment. One remaining question. "Golfing seems to be a male-dominated sport, a he-man's domicile. But women have successfully invaded the golf courses in recent years. Indeed, look at the success of the LPGA, which is coming to Tallahassee in a few weeks. Do you have any suggestions for the woman who wants to get started in this field?"

Quinn smiled lazily, and his eyes became hooded. "Sure. She should have her man take her along the next time he plays golf and let him teach her all he knows."

Sydney's snappy response caught Quinn off-guard. "Did your woman take you golfing and teach you all she knew, Quinn?"

The interview ended weakly, with Quinn mumbling, "Of course not. I learned the basics years ago and went to college on a scholarship. I meant that women or anyone should learn the basics first."

"I see." She closed with a warm thank you to Quinn Robinson, ex-professional golfer.

When the camera stopped, he exploded, "What the hell was the meaning of that? You made me look like a chauvinist!" He followed her out of the room, furious at the abrupt turn at the end of the interview. And after he'd been so easy on her, too.

"You made yourself look like a chauvinist. That was a shabby remark."

"I was only kidding!"

"Well, I wasn't. Don't you realize that women are tired of those kinds of put-downs?" She stopped in the hallway to face him.

"That was a low blow. I gave you straight answers throughout this whole interview, then you swung low at the very end!"

"It was a serious question. You gave a stupid answer that left you open for my comeback. Actually, I've done you a favor, Quinn. Just be thankful there'll be only thirty students and my professor who'll see this. Next time you'll be prepared."

"Prepared? Male interviewers don't ask that kind of question."

"That's because sports reporting is so male-dominated. But that's changing, too."

"Oh? Since when? You're the first female I've encountered who knew a sensible thing to ask about professional golfing."

"Is that so? Well, this should show you that neither golfing nor any other sport is a male bastion. It just takes a little nerve, but women are doing it."

"Is that it? A one-woman crusade to break down male barriers? First you hit me up with golfing. Then you tackle sports in general. Is that what you think you want?"

"I intend to be a sportscaster, and I think I've got what it takes." Her green eyes flashed determinedly at him.

"You've got what it takes, all right. To infuriate the poor slob you're supposed to be interviewing."

She blinked and took a shaky breath. He was right. She shouldn't have attacked him like that. In a real situation on TV, she might have lost her job.

"And another thing," he continued. "You'd better get used to the way men talk if you're going to storm their bastion. You shouldn't have stopped my story about the one that got away. I had a cute story to tell."

"I was in charge of the interview," she said firmly. "And I just guided it in the direction I wanted it to go. That's what I've been taught to do in this class."

"It wouldn't have taken more than a couple of minutes. Anyway, men like to hear fish tales," he objected stubbornly.

"Well, women don't. Anyway, I'd probably have been cheering for the fish, because I'd be on the side of the one that got away."

"What?"

One hand rose to prop on her slender hip. "How could you catch all those innocent little fish? You, with all your spiffy equipment, cam-reels, special lures, and depth-finders. You must have a helluva buildup of iodine in your body from eating so many fish."

"What the hell are you talking about?" He frowned at her impatiently. "I don't eat them. I don't even keep them. I release them when the day's catch is counted and weighed."

"You do?" Her jaw dropped. She was all set to berate him for depopulating the streams and lakes of this country.

"In all your research, didn't you find that out? It's the challenge that counts. Most of the fish are released back into the lake. Except the trophy fish, of course."

"Trophy? Aha! I knew it!" She wheeled away, envisioning the gory sight of at least a dozen openmouthed bass mounted in all their glory on Quinn's den walls. Why, his entire house must be full of them! She shuddered. What had ever made her think she knew this man? Much less, admired him!

39

"I don't eat them. Don't even like the taste of fish!" he called to her receding back. Quinn watched the gentle sway of her skirt as Sydney strode away from him. He knew what those lovely, long legs looked like —and he knew she was right. He'd been a fool to jump right into her feminist snare. And now, the more he said, the deeper he got. He was even so engrossed in their argument, he'd forgotten that she promised he'd have a spot on TV. "Sydney! Wait a minute."

When he reached her side, he conceded, "Maybe— maybe you're right. I answered like a fool, a chauvinist if you insist. And you did me a favor by pointing it out. I guarantee it won't happen again. Can a macho he-man apologize to a woman when he's wrong?"

She gave him a small smile. "Of course. I—I owe you an apology, too. I'm sorry I was so rough on you during the taping. You're right. I shouldn't antagonize a subject, no matter what he or she says. And I want to thank you again for doing the interview in the first place, Quinn. I didn't intend for it to end this way. Honest."

He shrugged. "Me either. Let me buy you a cup of coffee before we're through."

She dropped her eyes, then lifted them to meet the intensity of his. "Well, I—I suppose so. Sure."

They went to the campus coffee shop because it was most convenient. By nearly five thirty, the crowd had cleared out, and they practically had the place to themselves.

They sat in a booth, and a feeling of intimacy immediately shrouded them. Quinn ordered his coffee black. Sydney requested cream with hers. She folded her arms on the table, trying to appear calm. Inside,

40

though, she was quivering. Maybe it was because she hadn't been intimate with, or even interested in, a man for so long.

Quinn watched her and wondered about the wariness in her emerald eyes. He had seen her temper flare, but she wasn't being completely honest with him. She was holding back, hiding her past and perhaps her true nature. His natural curiosity made him want to explore her further. She had a sensuality about her, but in no way was she flirtatious. It was as if she really didn't want to attract him. Was that possible, for a healthy, single woman?

They didn't speak until the coffee was served, and even then Quinn initiated the conversation. "Tell me about yourself, Sydney. Why are you going back to school?"

She shrugged. "Why does anyone go to college? To get a degree."

"But why so late?"

"I'm only twenty-nine. That's hardly over the hill. After two years of college, I got married. I had to quit school and work to put my husband through school."

Quinn's gaze dropped to her ringless left hand. "But you're divorced now?"

"Yes. A year ago. I have a five-year-old son named Chad." Sydney smiled involuntarily as she spoke of her pride and joy. "Chad has blue eyes, is somewhat mischievous, and asks a million questions. What about you, Quinn? Married? Any kids?"

"Divorced. Like you." He studied her expression as he talked. For some reason, he wondered what she was thinking. Usually he didn't care what women thought about him. Usually he didn't bother to tell them any-

41

thing about his private life. Usually. "I have two daughters. Trina is seven; Lindi's six. They're great kids. They live with their mother in Lake City."

"How long have you been divorced?"

"Five years." He said it in an offhand way.

Sydney wondered if she'd ever be that blasé about her relationship with Daniel. Even though it had been over a year, and the end had been a long time coming, her wounds were still deep. Would she ever get over it? Would Chad?

"How has your divorce affected your daughters?" Sydney caught her breath and shook her head quickly. "I'm sorry, Quinn. That's much too personal. I shouldn't have asked you. It's just that being a single parent is so difficult at times."

Quinn detected a note of despair in her tone. For some reason, he was willing to share a part of his life with this woman. He wasn't sure why. "Quitting the pro golf circuit changed my life much more than the divorce did. Naturally it affected the girls. Believe it or not, I'm much more settled now. Stacey, my ex-wife, moved to Lake City, and we share custody. I take the girls every chance I get."

"Are they resentful because you don't have a conventional family life?"

"I don't think so. They seem to accept it. Things are a helluva lot better now than when I was actively playing golf. Stacey and I usually alternate having the kids on holidays."

Sydney pondered the prospects of sharing Chad with Daniel, perhaps losing him for the holidays. "I don't think I'd like that," she admitted candidly.

"Kids are amazing. They adjust much easier than

we adults. Someday I'll explain to them that the divorce was necessary."

A distant look filtered Sydney's eyes. "Yes, sometimes divorce is necessary. Has she remarried?"

"Stacey? No. She's—no."

It occurred to Sydney that it would probably be difficult to compare other men to the dynamic Quinn. "Quinn, I didn't mean to pry into your private life."

"That's all right. But let's talk about you. Tell me about this course you're taking. Is it part of a degree plan, or just a special interest?"

This was a much safer topic, and she entered it eagerly. "I'm finishing my degree in communications. I graduate in less than three weeks."

He looked at her with new regard. "I admire your ambition. Working, going to school, and being a single parent are a lot to juggle."

"I figure it'll be worth it someday. And soon." She paused to sip her coffee and gaze across the campus. "When I returned to college, I decided that the visual media is where I'd like to be."

"You know something, Sydney? I fully expect you to make it as a sportscaster. You have a spark in your eyes that says you don't give up." He leaned forward, his gaze sincere.

"Give up?" She smiled determinedly. "Oh, no. Not me."

"Someday I'll proudly say that Sydney Jacques was the first lady sportscaster to interview me."

"Thanks, Quinn." She laughed. "An hour ago, I thought you'd want to forget the whole thing ever happened."

43

"Never!" he vowed. "It was even worth the risk of getting mowed down in the sports store."

She laughingly shook her finger at him. "Oh, come on now. You said you'd forget about that."

His rakish grin lifted her heart. "It was one of those experiences you chalk up and laugh about in years to come."

Sydney's breath caught in her throat. *Years to come? Will I know you, Quinn Robinson, in years to come?* "As long as you don't hold grudges." She shifted and began to dig in her purse. "Right now, though, I need to rescue my baby-sitter from Chad. She likes for him to be gone by dinnertime."

"No, please. I'll get the tab," he objected vehemently. "I'm an old-fashioned man who wouldn't think of letting a lady pay for coffee. Chauvinists always pay, don't they?"

"You aren't old-fashioned, Quinn," Sydney laughed, dumping a handful of change onto the table. "You're Neanderthal! Anyway, the lady insists, as a token of thanks for the interview. And for the conversation." *For giving me some answers when I needed them.*

"Next time it's on me," he promised, flicking something from his billfold. "Here's my card. I'll be back in town next week. Call me when you get the TV spot set up." His eyes caught hers decisively.

"TV spot?" she repeated weakly. "Oh, yes." Sydney took the card reluctantly. It committed her to him again, obligated her to something she wasn't even sure she could deliver. But she'd promised. "I'll—I'll be in touch, Quinn."

"Sydney, I've enjoyed it."

"Thanks for what you said about your daughters

44

adjusting to your divorce. It helped." She stood up. Already she'd said too much.

"Sydney—"

She shook her head to ward off his questions. "I've got to go."

His blue eyes penetrated, questioned, probed, but he said nothing.

Sydney turned to go.

Quinn's voice was a low command. "Sydney, come back."

She turned back around, her eyes bound to his.

"Have dinner with me tonight."

"No, I can't."

"Meet me tonight, Sydney. Please. Just to talk. As friends."

Friends? The way she felt right now, the way he looked at her, friendship was the farthest thing from her mind. "No, I don't think so." She shook her head.

"Why? What are you running from?"

"Nothing!"

"Just dinner." His words were simple, his inference clear. "Can you get a sitter for Chad for a couple of hours?"

She shrugged and looked away. Oh, dear God, she wanted, no, needed, to talk with someone. "I—yes, probably."

"We'll go to Shadow's. It's quiet. Secluded."

"And romantic?" she grated and met his gaze again. She didn't want that. Not now. She wasn't ready.

"It's a good place for friends to meet. And talk. Nothing more." His hand closed over her wrist, and her pulse throbbed beneath his warm, tender touch. "You need a friend, don't you, Sydney?"

"Yes." Her voice was a bare whisper. For a man who worked outdoors, his hands were remarkably soft and gentle. His thumb drew slow circles over her wrist, and she wanted to feel that magic touch all over. Slow and gentle and sensuous. "I do need a friend." Dear God, she was weak.

"I'm offering. See you tonight at eight."

He moved his hand, and she was free to go. Sydney looked down at the wrist, half-expecting it to show the fiery imprint of his hand, but it looked normal. "All right." Before she had time to regret it, she gave him her address, then quickly walked away.

Quinn watched her go, his arms folded on the table. A strange tightness knotted in his chest. What was this woman doing to him? It was greater than either of them, this attraction they couldn't resist. He could feel it, almost as if it were something tangible.

It wouldn't hurt to see her just this once. But the last thing in the world he needed right now was a woman to complicate his life.

Sydney returned home, filled with such mixed emotions, she could barely think straight. She popped a frozen pizza into the oven for Chad, then called Lora.

"I need a sitter tonight. An—old friend is in town and wants to have dinner. Would you be a dear and keep Chad?" She carefully avoided mentioning whether the "friend" was male or female. "I won't be late."

"Unfortunately, I have absolutely nothing planned tonight, honey. Randy is working late, and I would love to sit with Chad. In fact, if it'll help, I'll come over to your house. That way, I can put Chad to bed in his own room."

"Lora, you're wonderful. I owe you one."

"Um-hum. How about introducing me to a fabulously wealthy man who'll sweep me off my feet?"

"You're talking fantasy, Lora. That only happens in books. They don't make real ones like that."

"Oh yes, they do. It's just that they're hidden in the deep recesses of the South American jungles. Or all taking cruises on the Love Boat."

"So what are we doing here in Tallahassee?"

"Damned if I know! You just have a good time tonight, Sydney. You deserve it. When do you want me there?"

"A little before eight."

"Will do. See you then."

Sydney sighed as she replaced the phone. Why had she said yes to Quinn? The last thing she wanted—needed—was involvement with a man right now. Why, she was still attached to Daniel. It was an umbilical cord she longed to clip. And she was determined it would happen soon.

Now certainly wasn't the time to become involved with another man. Her independence had been too hard to come by, and it was so close now that she could taste it. It was a sweetness she wanted to savor.

But then, Quinn Robinson's smile had an appeal she couldn't resist.

CHAPTER THREE

Quinn slid down into the Jacuzzi, letting the force of the jets work their sensuous magic on the entire length of his bare body. He was rigid and tense, an unusual state for him. Years ago, he'd abandoned tension-creating stress factors along with their accompanying lifestyle. In an effort to get back in control of his body tonight, he willed his muscles to relax and allow the foaming water to do its job and tranquilize him. Usually, it worked. But tonight was different. He couldn't get his mind off that woman.

Sydney Jacques.

Quinn lowered himself until he was completely submerged in the swirling water. The Jacuzzi's motor hummed in his ears, blocking out all other sounds, any remaining thoughts. *Everything but her image.* Like a miniature tanned whale, he surfaced, blowing and splattering water. The waves created by the thrust of his body surged back and forth, spilling the balmy liquid over the sides and onto the Italian-tiled bathroom floor.

"Damn!" He grabbed a thick towel and threw it onto the growing puddle.

What was it about this woman that was different

from others? Those green eyes! That was it! She'd be-witched him with eyes as green as the deepest river. Oh, he was under some kind of spell, all right. Why couldn't he just leave town tomorrow and forget her? Why did he have to insist on seeing her tonight?

Forget her?

Forget those emerald eyes? They were like sensuous jewels, beckoning him. Dismiss those long, going-on-forever legs? Hardly! Quinn had always liked long legs on a woman, but this one had fabulous limbs! Straight and long and firm. Lightly tanned. Athletic, but not too muscular. What would it be like to caress them? He ran a wet hand over the planes of his face. He had to stop thinking of her like this. After all, she'd made it perfectly clear that she had no romantic interest in him.

Maybe I could change her mind.

How could he dismiss her rich, slightly unruly mane of hair? Its unusual auburn color was so inviting. Dark, with flecks of gold. How he wanted to bury his hands in it, wanted to bring a smile to those sad green eyes.

Was it possible to change her mind? He'd been per-suasive about dinner tonight by convincing her they'd just be friends. And she had believed him.

But he had lied.

With a low moan, Quinn reached for the bar of soap. Distractedly, he scrubbed over every part of his body with his soapy palm.

Even when Quinn's tension-racked body was thor-oughly cleansed, his efforts to wash Sydney away from his mind were futile. He flipped the drain switch and heaved himself out of the Jacuzzi. A cursory effort with the thick towel left his tanned body still glistening with moisture beads. He dropped the towel and swished the rumpled heap around on the floor with his foot a couple of times.

Then, like a caged lion, he stalked the confines of his house. Still nude, Quinn reached into the refrigerator and grasped a beer. He walked through the living room and stood before the uncurtained double French doors, drinking the beer, lost in thought.

It wasn't quite dark, yet the moon was visible, a crystalline crescent in a murky, plum-colored sky. It hung low on the horizon, as if threatening to drop into the lake. In the backyard, the aquamarine swimming pool shone in evening's growing curtain as an occasional highlight sparked its surface.

Quinn opened the door and moved boldly outside with no thought about his nudeness. The lean, hard lines of his masculine body glowed with the vigor of an athlete. His palm moved unconsciously across his flat-muscled belly, where the dark hair trail led to an untanned bikini triangle.

He frowned. What drew him to this troubled woman with the deep green eyes, when he could have almost any other woman he wanted?

Ah, that was it! He wanted Sydney Jacques. There was no denying it. He was a man with a strong libido, and he desired this woman. And when she didn't return the desire, she became a challenge.

Quinn sat for a long time, clothed only in darkness, his sinewy muscles once again rigid and tense. Finally, near seven thirty, he went inside to dress for dinner. As he slid skintight briefs over his taut hips, he promised himself not to take her seriously.

* * *

When Sydney opened the door that night, all Quinn's doubts and promises to himself flew out the window. She was stunning, and he wanted her in his arms more than ever. A weak, possibly nervous, smile greeted him, and he was struck by the aura of vulnerability about her. She was dressed casually in an emerald blouse and white slacks and stood with her head held high. Proud. Defensive. Slightly haughty. But he could see pain in her eyes. Or was he reading too much into them?

They stood motionless for an uncomfortable second, eyes meeting in a mesmerizing bond. Then Quinn broke it. "Ready to go?"

She nodded and stepped outside into the hallway. Before she closed the apartment door, they could hear the TV in the background and Chad's small voice talking to Lora.

Quinn was careful not to touch her, but oh how he wanted to caress those shoulders, to take her hand reassuringly, to capture her face. To bring a smile to those perfect lips.

They spoke very little in the car. The shadows of night had created a strange mood for them. Serene. Beautiful. Romantic. It was something neither of them wanted nor expected. Gone was the soft, humorous banter. Neither could think of anything light to say, so they sat in silence.

At the restaurant, the hostess seated them in the back, a quiet, out-of-the-way table. Here they could talk in lovely privacy. But they had nothing to say. Then they both spoke at once.

"Sydney, we—"

51

"Quinn, I—"

"Go ahead," he deferred with a polite hand motion.

She took a deep breath. "I have to say that coming here tonight was probably a mistake. I don't know why I agreed to it. Desperately lonely, I guess. A little crazy, maybe. Or both. But if you think anything else will come of this evening, just forget it. I'm here for dinner, possibly friendship, and nothing else." She had worked herself into a fair lather over the little speech, and pink spots burned at her cheeks.

"Are you finished?" he grated.

Sydney nodded, defiance still alight in her eyes.

"Then let me straighten you out, Ms. Jacques. I figure that one of the stupidest things I've ever done was coming here tonight. I thought long and hard about it and damn near didn't show! The last thing in the world I need to do is get involved with a woman, especially one who has your sarcastic attitude." His blue eyes flashed harshly over her, the humor and softness in them gone.

"Are *you* finished?" she retorted.

He nodded curtly. "That's all I have to say about the matter."

They glared at each other for a full minute, the anger and frustration in both of them surfacing, the feelings spilling over. Although it might be disastrous, Quinn was relieved they'd gotten those frustrations out in the open.

Sydney's voice gentled ever so slightly. "Then why *did* you show up?"

"I don't know." He shrugged, and his blue eyes softened faintly. "Why did you come?"

She shrugged, too, her lips forming a tight smile. "Crazy, I guess."

"Do you want to leave? It isn't too late."

"Do you want to?"

A waiter appeared and stood formally by their table, uncomfortably aware that he had interrupted something strained between the couple. "Excuse me, sir. Would you and the lady like a cocktail before dinner?"

"What do you think?" Quinn addressed her, his eyes answering her question.

Sydney studied the intricately folded napkin that rested beside her plate. This was her chance, her time to say politely, "No, thanks, we were just leaving."

She looked back up at Quinn's intense blue eyes and knew she couldn't leave, not yet. She was here because she wanted to be; perhaps because she needed to be. "I'll have a Chablis."

Quinn tried to mask the relief that flooded his face, as if it didn't matter. But it did matter, and that showed in the warmth of his eyes. "The lady will have a glass of Chablis. Make mine a Scotch and water."

When the waiter left, Quinn leaned forward. "I know this sounds half-baked, but if you'd decided to leave, I'm afraid I would have camped on your doorstep."

She smiled at the touch of his old humor. "Why?"

"Simple. Tomorrow I'm leaving town, and I'll be gone all week and—" His voice trailed and he paused. "I think I'm bewitched by your green eyes. There's something I just have to know about them. You don't wear contacts, do you? Those colored ones that change gray eyes to bright blue? Or hazel eyes to deep green?"

"No, these are really mine. Is that all you needed to know? You certainly wouldn't have had to camp on my doorstep to find that out."

"That isn't all." He shook his head tightly and waited for their drinks to be served. He tipped his glass to hers. "Salud." Their eyes met again, and they sipped their drinks quietly for a few moments.

"You were saying," she reminded him, "that the truth about my eyes isn't all you need to know."

"Right. That's just for starters. Sydney, you must know you're a damned good-looking woman, and I'm not blind to that. In fact, I'm downright attracted to you. Now, if you should change your mind about being friends and wanted to consider being lovers, I wouldn't object a bit."

Her green eyes flared across the table. "You split-tongued devil! I thought you said you didn't want to get involved with me. Friends, you promised."

"I don't. Becoming lovers wouldn't have to make us involved."

"It wouldn't?"

"Nah," he drawled lazily. "Friends can be lovers and not let it get serious. Not if they don't want it to be. And we've both already established that."

"We have?" She stared at the man with growing amazement.

"Sure. The trick is just to establish the ground rules early. Then stick to them."

"Ground rules?" she nettled. "Sounds simple enough. Trouble is, I don't go to bed with a man that easily."

"Then maybe I can change your mind," he offered readily.

"I doubt it," she murmured sardonically. Seduction was what he had in mind. She should have realized it sooner. So why didn't she just get up and leave now? Sydney's green eyes snapped at him across the table, but she remained seated. Perhaps it was the challenge of his banter that kept her there. Perhaps the alluring blue of his eyes.

"Quinn, this is the strangest conversation I've ever had. A minute ago, we were considering leaving. Talking about how we nearly didn't come here tonight. Now we're discussing becoming lovers."

He grinned crookedly. "See how easily we get along? I wouldn't have even mentioned it, but I could see that we just hit it right off. We go together easily, like biscuits and honey. Trouble is, neither of us wants a confining relationship. As long as we each understood that, it would be okay. No one would get hurt. That'd be part of the ground rules."

"Strange ground rules, Quinn. Most men want to possess."

"Most women want a commitment."

"I've had that. It doesn't work."

Quinn's eyes caressed her face. Oh, how he wanted to cover that ivory skin with kisses. So *that* was the source of her pain: a commitment that hadn't worked. "Possession doesn't work, either. Actually, both possession and commitment are confining. I'd rather have you of your own free will, Sydney. The key word there is *free*. You see, I travel a lot. I wouldn't want to be unreasonably confining to you."

She smiled, easily following his logic. "And you want to be free, too."

He shrugged. "Freedom is a two-way street. It could be good for both of us. Then, too, it's always nice to think you have a friend and lover to rely on. I mean, I'm a handy man to have around. I can change a tire, plunge a toilet, or repair the roof. All you'd have to do is give a call."

"And whenever you wanted someone to warm your bed, you'd just give me a call," she grated with raised eyebrows.

He pursed his lips. "I'm not a demanding man, Sydney. Remember, I said we'd operate on a free-will basis. I'd want you to want to be there."

She gave him a doubtful smile, and he continued in a low, persuasive voice. "Surely there are times when you want a man to hold you. To love you."

Her smile faded. Where was the humor that usually softened his words? Was he still teasing? It had been a strange conversation, and she was now caught off-guard. "Yes, sometimes," she whispered.

"I thought so."

The waiter returned, and they ordered steak and salad. For some reason, conversation came more easily. So did the laughter during dinner.

As they finished, Quinn asked, "Have you given some thought to my proposal?"

"Proposition would be a better word for it," Sydney countered. "I must say, Quinn, this is the most unorthodox conversation I've ever had. I hardly know you."

"Knowing me isn't as important as trusting me."

"Why should I trust you, Quinn Robinson?"

56

He smiled boyishly and shrugged. "I have an honest face."

"Yes, you do. It has nice angles. A strong chin line."

"And you have nice legs."

"What?"

"We're being honest, aren't we?"

"Are we, Quinn?"

"Absolutely!"

"Then why do I feel like I don't know you at all?"

"I thought you found out everything about me in your research. You know what my hobbies are and where I live. You know I'm divorced and have two daughters who live with their mother nearby in Lake City. You probably even know how much money I make each year on advertising. What more do you need to know?"

"Before we become lovers?" She laughed.

"Before we know if it works between us. It might not, you know. And that would be okay, too."

"Would it, Quinn?" She leaned forward. "Could we still be friends?"

"Of course."

"You're an unusual man, Quinn Robinson."

"I'm just an average man."

"I don't think so."

He shrugged outstretched hands. They were large hands, hands that were strong but gentle. Hands that worked for him, yet could caress with definite sensitivity. "I just enjoy myself."

"And quite profitably, if my research was correct."

"I can't complain."

She laughed, thinking of the striking differences in

their life-styles, their incomes. And yet at this moment, did it matter?

Quinn touched her hand. He loved the way her emerald eyes danced with flecks of gold and came to life when she laughed.

Self-consciously, she moved her hand from beneath his. "How did golfing become your career?"

"Right here at Florida State. I came here on a golfing scholarship and just kept on winning tournaments."

"You make it sound so easy, and I know it wasn't."

"I've swung a lot of golf clubs in my time. And I was lucky."

"Luck probably had very little to do with your success, Quinn. What made you quit?"

"Bad shoulder. Bursitis gave me constant pain the last few years I played. Then I had a crazy accident. Fell on some rocks trout fishing in Tennessee. Surgery didn't stop the pain, so I gave in. Quit. Now I'm free to pursue other avenues."

"Like women?"

"Like you. Not others."

"Why me, Quinn?"

"I told you. I like your legs. And you intrigue me, Sydney."

"There's more to me than my legs."

"I'm well aware of that. And I can't wait to get to the rest. I know you're a woman with a purpose. You have definite goals and are after them with a vengeance. I've never seen anyone with more drive."

"Any other observations?"

"You've been hurt. Badly. And I'd like to know

why." They finished the meal and ordered coffee. "Well, are you going to tell me about him?"

"About who?" She feigned ignorance and stirred cream into the dark coffee in her cup.

"Your ex-husband. Or whoever hurt you so badly."

"Quinn, this has been such a lovely evening. Even with the teasing about making love. I don't think you want to spoil it with my sorry epic."

"I told you about my shoulder. This is confession time. Yes, I do want to know about you." His eyes met hers levelly, and he was dead serious. "Was it the divorce?"

Sydney lifted sad green eyes. "I think the correct term for what happened is *desertion,*" she clipped bitterly. "Abandoned. When Daniel left, I didn't know where he was for two days."

"Deserted? You and his own kid?"

She nodded. "Chad was only four. I was frantic. I was going to school and didn't have a job. Had no way to pay the bills. The police wouldn't touch it. Said a husband who left a note before skipping town wasn't a police matter, it was a domestic problem."

"So what did you do?"

"I waited like a good little wife until he called to reassure me that he hadn't been dumped in the river and to announce that he wouldn't be coming home anymore. Eventually, I filed for divorce. I guess I'm still picking up the pieces."

"Daniel sounds like a first-class jackass. How could a man just leave his wife and son?"

"He had problems he couldn't handle. His solution was to dump them. And us."

"And dump everything in your lap?"

59

"Things were pretty bad for a while. I had become very dependent on him. Obviously that wasn't good for either of us."

Quinn's eyes narrowed. "Are you making excuses for him?"

She looked down, then lifted her chin. "No. But I feel I wasn't the wife I should have been, or this wouldn't have happened."

"Ridiculous! I can't imagine you being—"

"Well, imagine it. I had become increasingly dependent on him for everything, not just financially. He was my emotional support, my shoulder to cry on, my big brother, my father, my best friend, and, eventually, the father of my son. Apparently, it was too much for him."

"I don't understand you, Sydney. This doesn't sound like the ardent feminist who raked me over the coals this afternoon on tape."

She wrapped her fingers around the warm coffee cup. "This is the real me, somewhere between a clinging vine and a hard-hearted Hannah."

"You sound like a woman who's been hurt. Very badly." Quinn's hand reached for hers. This time she didn't pull away, and the fiery attraction was like a spark welding them together. Oh, how he wanted more. He wanted to take her in his arms, soothe her worried brow, make her forget the man who'd hurt her so.

"Don't feel sorry for me. I'm going to make it now," she said with quiet assurance. "I'll graduate from college in three weeks, and then I'll have a decent job. I can be independent for the first time in my life. It's very important to me."

"That's why that interview today was so crucial."

Sydney nodded and finished off her coffee. "I have to get a good job. Chad and I are completely dependent on me."

"I don't see how you can miss. That was a dynamite interview. You had me going in the direction you wanted." Still do, he mused.

She smiled wryly. "You didn't think so this afternoon."

"I also didn't think much of you almost hitting me in the head with a golf ball yesterday, but that doesn't mean your swing wasn't perfect!"

"It was a lucky shot," she acknowledged with a laugh.

"Missing me?"

"Meeting you."

Quinn squeezed her hand. When they left the restaurant, his arm went naturally around her shoulders. She didn't protest. There was a gentle magnetism between them, warm and cozy. *Just friends,* he tried to warn himself, yet he wished . . .

At her apartment door, Sydney smiled. "I'm surprised you didn't pressure me tonight. About your proposition."

"Then you aren't entirely opposed to the idea?"

She shrugged with a smile. It was a crazy notion.

"I understand," he said gently. "I want you to have time to think about it. Plus, we have to see if it would work."

"Oh? And how do we do that?"

"Like this." He lowered his head, his lips matching hers with warm pressure. Tiny moist kisses caressed her lips with sensuality until the motion was one deep, compelling drink of intoxicating passion. His fingers laced into her hair, trembling with the desire to rake over every part of her.

He raised his head, then bent to kiss her once again. "I think it might work. In time."

"It might, in time," she agreed weakly. With a soft "See you," she disappeared into her small home.

Quinn sighed raggedly. Right now, he had to be content with keeping his distance from this woman. He thought of spending the next week out of town. Without her.

It was the first time in years he'd wanted a woman he couldn't have.

CHAPTER FOUR

"Okay, Chad. You just run along, as fast as you can, and let the wind take your kite up, up, up to the clouds!" Sydney flapped one arm for emphasis and waggled her homemade held-together-with-glue kite with the other. "Watch me."

Chad nodded solemnly. To him, it was serious business. A whiff of a faint breeze rustled through his Godzilla-face kite, also homemade. "Better hurry, Mom. The wind's coming."

Sydney glanced up at the clear blue sky. Not a cloud in sight. It didn't occur to her that there wasn't a breeze up there, either.

"And we've got to catch it!" She whirled around and took off across the field, kite arm extended, praying for a stiff breeze. It was a calm, warm, lazy Tallahassee day.

Puffing her way across the entire length of the football field, Sydney looked up at the limp kite. It dangled at the end of her hand, its tail dragging at her heels. "Fly, you stupid thing!"

That was the last she remembered until she looked up into the fuzzy face of a man.

"You all right?"

Sydney groaned. *Oh God . . . can't breathe . . . going to die . . . hit by a huge boulder . . . pressing down hard . . . hurting . . . move the boulder so I can breathe . . . CAN'T BREATHE!*

She gasped frantically—but no air reached her lungs. Panic surged through her, and she struggled to get up. Desperately she fought for air. Large hands pushed her back down flat. No air! The boulder pressing on her lungs was growing! Heavy and hard. Hurting. A man's hand dug into the front of her jeans. And lifted her hips with her waistband.

"Easy now. Breathe easy. It's coming back. You're all right, Syd. Just take little breaths. Easy now. You got the wind knocked out of you, that's all. You're going to be okay."

The voice was calm and soothing, and she tried to obey and take shallow breaths. In another second, precious air reached her aching lungs. She gulped large doses of the glorious stuff and blinked away the fuzziness. More air, and the faces circled around her took definite shape and became recognizable. Chad, his small face concerned. And the man with the soothing voice and his hand in her jeans—Quinn Robinson.

"Oh-h-h. What—what are you doing?"

"Helping you get your breath. This does something with your diaphragm and lungs."

"I'm better now. Thanks. Put me down."

He lowered her hips to the ground. "And what were you doing?"

She felt his fingers trail along her belly as he released her. "Helping Chad fly a kite."

"Like that, Mom?"

"No, honey. Not quite." She struggled to a sitting

64

position and realized there were two faces staring at her besides Chad's and Quinn's. Little girls with long blond hair and big blue eyes, like Quinn's.

"Sydney, I want you to meet my daughters." Quinn drew them closer to the circle. "Lindi and Trina. The lady with the kite wrapped around her is Sydney Jacques. And I presume this is Chad?"

"Yep, that's me."

Sydney smiled wanly at the two cherubic faces. She felt weak and as limp and inept as her kite. "Yes, this is my son, Chad. Nice to meet you, Lindi, Trina."

Quinn helped her to her feet, and the children gathered up the kite scraps.

"Is that all, Mom? Are we quitting? Before I even get my kite off the ground?"

Sydney sighed. "Well, honey, Mom's not up to—"

"Of course not," Quinn answered enthusiastically. "We're just starting! I'll help you get your kite off the ground, Chad. I've had some experience with this. Girls, go get your kites, and we'll have fun with Chad. After we park Sydney under a tree. And bring her a Coke, will you, Trina? She could probably use a little lift."

"Coke?" Chad repeated.

"Sure," Trina answered. "They're in our refrigerator. Want one?"

"Yeah!" Chad stopped and looked at Sydney. "Can I, Mom?"

"Your refrigerator? How?" She looked at Quinn.

"In the camper. Makes it easier if we just bring our own," he said casually. "Would you rather have a Sprite?"

"Can I, Mom? Please?"

"Coke is fine," Sydney said, and nodded vaguely at Chad.

"Yahoo!" Chad took off with the girls, and Sydney's gaze followed them all the way to the sleek thirty-foot motor home.

"Camper?" she drawled.

Quinn shrugged. "It's accommodating. Makes it easier to camp and haul the girls and all their stuff around."

"Oh sure, I should have known. You have a different vehicle for each time of day. And every event."

"Why not?" He chuckled and led her to the sidelines, his arm wrapped securely around her shoulder.

"Your children are beautiful, Quinn."

"Thanks. I agree. They take after their mother."

"They have their father's eyes." Sydney halted and caught his blue gaze. His eyes were enchanting. "So does Chad. Have his father's eyes, I mean."

"He's a good-looking kid. Like his mother." He motioned toward the motor home. "Trina's seven and just at that age where she thinks she's in charge. She'll probably smother Chad, hovering over him like a little mother hen."

Sydney smiled warmly. "He'll love the attention. Sometimes I feel guilty because I have to leave him so much."

"Now, Lindi's more his age and will probably give him a run for his money."

"A little competition will be good for him. They're darling, Quinn."

"They're very special to me."

"I can tell. I know what you mean, Quinn. Sometimes I feel responsible to make up for both parents because Chad's father isn't around."

Quinn's mouth tightened, and Sydney remembered how those lips caressed hers. "You can't be both. Don't try. Just be yourself. He'll understand. And he'll make it fine as long as he knows you love him."

"Well, of course, he knows that." Sydney looked up as the three children ran toward them, clutching Cokes and elaborate kites. The girl's kites were lightweight plastic with colorful designs, three-dimensional shapes, and long, braided tails. Nothing homemade about them. They were exquisite—and expensive.

After settling Sydney under a shade tree, Quinn took the kids out to the middle of the football field and soon had them flying their kites higher than the treetops. Sydney sipped the icy Coke and watched them play. Quinn was fascinating, and fun. He threw himself into the project, joining the kids' play with fervor. Their delightful laughter filled the air as their kites fought for supremacy.

Eventually, he left them to their own games, grabbed a Coke from the motor home, and joined Sydney.

"Whew! Those kids can wear a man out!"

"You kept up with them pretty well, Quinn. Thank you for helping me with Chad's kite."

"We had fun." Quinn said it with such conviction, Sydney had no choice but to believe him.

"Quinn, why are you here?"

His blue gaze settled on her like a warm cloak. "I knew you'd be here, playing with Chad. I figured it would be a good place to bring the girls. And"—he tossed a small stick into the grass—"I wanted to see you again."

"I thought you were going out of town. Fishing."

"Stacey—that's my ex—called last night. She had an emergency with her dad and needed help with the girls. I told her to bring them down."

"You canceled your plans?"

"Sure. They're my kids. When they need me, I'm available. They won't always need me. But they do now."

"I admire you, Quinn. It's hard for some fathers to do this." She was thinking with bitterness that Chad's father had only spent a couple of days with him since the divorce.

"My girls are special, Syd, and I'd do anything I could for them."

"They're lucky to have a father like you."

"I don't know about lucky, but they're stuck with me." He pointed with a laugh. "Whoops! Lindi's kite got tangled with Chad's. I'd better go try to salvage something before those kids rip them apart."

While he straightened out the kites, Sydney decided that Quinn Robinson was someone very special and that no one, especially children, would ever be stuck with him.

They all returned, dragging kites and talking excitedly. "We took a vote, Syd." Quinn stood amid the three blue-eyed children, his expression every bit as youthful as theirs. "It's hot dogs for lunch and double-dip ice cream cones afterward. How do you vote?"

Sydney gaped at the quartet. Trina clutched Chad's hand protectively and nodded with a smile. Lindi's small face glowed, fully expecting agreement. And

68

then there was Chad, waiting anxiously for her answer.

"You don't have to go to work again today, do you, Mom? Oh, please. We're having such fun."

Her heart twisted, and Sydney knew that even if she had been scheduled to work, she would have canceled today. "Sure. It's been ages since I've had a hot dog."

"Yeah!" The kids yelled happily and made a dash for the motor home.

"You sure you want to do this?" Sydney questioned Quinn.

"Sure, I'm sure. Never been more sure. That is, if you're sure you want to do this." He pulled her to her feet and held her hand as they ran after the kids.

"Why did I ask?" she groaned spiritedly and stumbled along.

They were a rowdy, laughing bunch, eating hot dogs and dripping catsup and chili and teasing each other about who made the biggest mess. The girls demonstrated that they had inherited some of their father's sense of humor and zest for life, for they quickly adopted Sydney and Chad into their amiable circle.

They ended up at a wild and wacky ice cream parlor, sitting in candy-striped chairs and joking with the clown waiters. Smiling, Sydney watched Chad's valiant efforts at licking his double-dip cone. It was a skill he hadn't mastered yet, and drips of bubble-gum ice cream joined the catsup on his skirt.

"Having fun?"

She looked up and realized Quinn had been watching her. "Yes. It's been a wonderful day, Quinn. Chad has had a great time."

69

"I know Chad's enjoyed himself. One look at the mess on the front of his shirt explains all. How about you, Syd?"

She felt herself sinking into the aura of his blue eyes. "Me, too."

"I'm glad. I don't want it to end, Sydney. You're easy to be around. And game for the kid's antics. Some adults find that difficult."

"You forget I was one myself." She laughed.

"Sometimes I think I still am," he admitted with a chuckle. "A kid trapped in a man's body."

"Sounds like a Disney movie plot," she said. "I don't want it to end, either, but I'm afraid Chad and I need to be getting back home. It's Saturday, and I have a million things to do before next week's finals."

"Don't let it end, Sydney. Make it an evening at my place. We can rent a movie for the kids and fix hamburgers on the grill."

"Well, I—"

"Don't forget to put an extra hamburger on for Mommy. She's staying for supper," Trina reminded Quinn.

"Oh, sure." Quinn gave her a quick nod. "Well, how about it, Syd? Can we count on you and Chad?"

Sydney quickly read into Trina's remark and knew she didn't want to be around if Quinn's ex was there. He probably didn't want her there, either, but was stuck with the invitation. "Thanks for inviting us, Quinn. But we can't. We really need to go."

He shook his head as if trying to figure her out. "I'll take you back to your car." He stood up and steered the kids to the motor home. While the girls showed Chad every secret drawer and how many beds were

70

hidden in the back, Quinn drove around the block in silence.

He pulled to a stop behind her old Chevy and tried again. "No strings attached, Syd. Promise. Why don't you and Chad come on out?" His blue eyes twinkled, and she remembered his easy proposition about making love when they needed it. No strings attached.

"I never did go for that idea, anyway, Quinn."

"The kids make everything different, Syd. I wouldn't—"

"Oh, Daddy!" Lindi rushed up to the front seat and threw her arms around Quinn. "That man's selling balloons that float! Can I have one?"

"Lindi, don't interrupt. It isn't polite."

"They don't float. They have special air that makes them stand up," Trina informed them.

"Do too float," Lindi insisted, pointing. "See?"

"You're both right. They're filled with helium gas and that makes them float. Here. Get one for everybody." He handed Lindi a five-dollar bill and tried to return his attention to Sydney.

"Daddy?" Lindi's small hand grasped his chin and turned his face. "Daddy, can I get one for my friend Beth?"

"I don't care."

"Thanks, Daddy. She's sick and this balloon will make her feel better."

"Great. Now, go." He looked at Sydney. "I'll just be in town tomorrow. Course, I'll have the kids, but you can bring Chad, and we can let them play on the lake and—"

"Daddy, can we stop by and take Beth her balloon?"

71

He sighed heavily. "Lindi, you're interrupting again."

"Sorry, Daddy, but this is important. Beth is in the hospital and I want—"

"Yes. Yes, whatever you want. We'll stop by and see Beth."

"Daddy, you're the greatest!" She squeezed him tightly with small arms, then clamored down the motor-home steps waving the five-dollar bill. The other two children scampered after her.

Quinn looked at Sydney.

She smiled encouragingly. "You're a patient man, Quinn."

"Only with the kids. With you, I'm impatient. I want to see you again. We'll be very disappointed if you can't make it. Sure you can't rearrange something?"

"No, I really can't. Maybe another time, Quinn."

"Like when?"

"I don't really know, Quinn."

He shrugged. "Okay, okay. I can tell when I'm getting the brush-off."

"Oh no, Quinn. I didn't mean—" She gripped his forearm, then looked down at her hand clutching him. Her fingers dug sensuously into the curly hairs on his arm. Instantly he covered her hand with his. It felt warm and strong, and she wanted to curl up in his arms as Lindi had done.

"Good. Then I'll call you when I get back in town."

She paused and felt the pulsing of her heart in her throat. "Okay. I'd like that, Quinn."

He leaned forward and kissed her lips quickly, then

backed off at the sounds of rambunctious youngsters approaching.

"Daddy! Daddy, look what color—"

"Later, Syd," he promised with a wink. He turned his attention to his daughter.

Sydney endured the next week, trying not to let Quinn Robinson monopolize her thoughts, never quite succeeding. She plowed through finals at school. At the last meeting of her interviewing class, the professor ran selected tapes. Her interview with Quinn was one of those chosen.

Mesmerized as she watched, Sydney hung onto his every word, observing his hands and the masculine way he sat and his devilish blue eyes. As the film ended, she realized that neither of them had been relaxed and natural that day. She saw none of the real Quinn on that tape, his humor, his warmth, his charm, his wonderful way with children.

"Miss Jacques? Did you want to speak to me about something?"

Sydney started and looked around. The classroom was empty. Dr. Goldbloom was stacking books in a box.

"Oh, yes. I just wanted to say that I enjoyed the class very much, Dr. Goldbloom. Thank you. I learned a lot, too." Flushed, she hurried away.

Home was no better. Chad rambled constantly about what fun they had had at the park last Saturday. And how quickly Quinn had gotten Godzilla to fly. And how the girls had shared Cokes with him, even given him one of the box kites for his very own.

"Wonder if I could put Godzilla in the box and fly both at the same time?" Chad asked.

"I'm sure Quinn could figure out a way," Sydney muttered absently as she set a plate of macaroni and cheese before him.

"Do you think so? Let's call him and see! We could meet them at the park again next week, Mom!"

"No! Just eat, Chad. And hush." She walked out of the kitchen feeling like a first-class heel. How could she squelch his enthusiasm like that? She hadn't seen Chad so animated and excited in a long time. And yet she thought she'd scream if she heard any more about Quinn Robinson. She had to get him out of her mind.

At work, she tried to remain steady, calm, and professional. After all, she was graduating soon, and that meant a chance for a real job. No more internship; no more gofer this and gofer that. She had submitted an updated job application, printing *sportscaster* on the dotted line with a small prayer, and had scheduled a private interview with the station manager next week.

Presently, though, she had to be content to be communications assistant.

"Sydney, please bring that documentary info to the meeting. It's in the bottom drawer of my desk."

"Sure, Margarite." Sydney retrieved the folder and slipped into a corner seat for the "specials" meeting. Each month, the station ran a couple of series of interest to the local community. Usually it involved political issues or candidates. Sometimes it was a human interest story featuring a local contest winner or hero. Sydney favored those stories.

Margarite called them "soft stuff," with a tone of disdain. Attractive, blond Margarite Mannville was

74

the nightly news co-anchor. The female half. There had been three male halves in the last four years. Difficult to work with, Margarite wielded a tremendous amount of power around the station. The only one who would dare oppose her was Lee Coffelt, the assistant station manager.

Sydney liked Lee but worried about his boldness with Margarite. That woman spelled trouble, and Lee didn't seem to care. He argued with her constantly because she wanted her hand in almost everything that went on the air.

"I could do a story about fear of the tse-tse fly invasion," Margarite offered.

"Too dull. Who cares?" Lee paced behind his chair.

"Fruit growers, that's who!"

"It's old news, Margarite. We've run the tse-tse fly into the ground—uh, so to speak."

Margarite leafed through her file. "What about acquisition of park land along the interstate?"

"Dead issue."

"School bonds?"

"Premature. We'll run it next fall."

"Contaminated groundwater?"

"Stinks! We've done it. Anybody else got any ideas? Something lighter than crime in the streets and what to do about the homeless." He went around the table, assessing contributions from the others. When he got to Sydney, he halted and surprised everyone. "Sydney? You got a suggestion?"

"Who, me?" He'd never asked her opinion about anything.

"You're graduating soon, aren't you? Show us what you've learned at the big university."

She tried not to stammer as all eyes went to her. "Well, uh, what about something to do with the upcoming golf tournaments? We have a Charity Pro and the LPGA. It would be news-related yet light."

Lee pursed his lips. "Yeah. Sounds good. Like what?"

"Well, like an interview with a retired pro golfer who lives here in Tallahassee."

"Retired golfer?" groaned Margarite. "Talk about dull!"

"The one I'm thinking about hasn't been retired long. And he isn't dull."

"Who, Syd?"

"Quinn Robinson."

"Yeah, well, chalk him off. I've tried for several years to get something going with that guy, but he's off limits. Very private. Couldn't care less about publicity." Lee waved one hand in a futile gesture.

"I think I could get him to do something for us."

"Not a chance, Syd. Good idea, though. Let's go with something on tung nuts unless something better comes along."

Margarite rolled her eyes. "Oh God, I'll bet we get tons of fan mail on that one. Let Sydney do the research. I'll narrate." She folded her materials and filed out with the group, grumbling with the production manager.

When everyone else had gone, Sydney approached the assistant station manager. "I'm sure I could get Quinn Robinson to do an interview, Lee."

"You're sure? What is he? A personal friend?" He eyed her narrowly.

Could you call someone who taught your son to fly

a kite and who shared a hot dog and ice cream cone and a perfectly lovely Saturday with his kids a personal friend? Someone who kissed like a dream? She nodded. "I know him. He even said—"

"Okay, Syd. See if you can get him to do it. If so, it's yours."

"M-mine? You mean—"

"Yeah. You do it. The interview, everything. You need something, don't you? Graduating? And looking for a job? Well, you need something on tape to show the boss. Reinhardt will want to see your work. Now you'll have something."

"Oh, Lee! You'd let me do this? What about Margarite? She'll be furious."

He gave Sydney a steady look. "I'll tell her it's about sports. That's your area of interest, leaving the hard news to her."

"Lee, you're terrific!"

He kept his usual reserve. "Let's see what you can do with this, Syd. I don't want a sitting-around-the-swimming-pool interview. I want a story about what he's doing now that he's retired. You know, something to interest people who followed his success for years. Maybe a little about the injury that caused him to retire. And what he's doing now. How does that sound?"

"Great, Lee! I'll do it! Thank you so much!"

"Just produce for me, Syd."

"I will! Oh, I will!"

She floated out of the office and called Quinn immediately. He'd just returned from the fishing trip. He'd had awful luck. Rained every day, so he cut it short. Great to hear from her. When could he see her again?

She replaced the receiver calmly and managed to keep her feet on the floor as she sailed into Lee's office. "He's agreed to do it next Friday!"

CHAPTER FIVE

On Friday, Sydney and Gary, the burly cameraman, followed Quinn around all day in the TV van. Quinn Robinson, they discovered, was a man of many talents and endless energy. A man who took his playing seriously.

Shortly after dawn, they stalked Quinn and two short-haired pointers. The dogs displayed their remarkable abilities to point birds and obey Quinn's hand directions. Noon found them at the country club, where Quinn conducted an hour-long golfing workshop. He treated them to a sumptuous lunch of Apalachicola oysters-on-the-half-shell and chilled lobster flown from the east coast. They were impressed. Later in the afternoon, they followed him home.

Home sweet home, Quinn Robinson style, was a contemporary structure by the lake with multicolored azaleas blooming everywhere and water oaks draped with Spanish moss lining the curved driveway—a gorgeous house by any standard.

"Get a shot of the house, Gary," Sydney instructed as they stepped out of the van, "while I do the standup."

"No. Don't take a picture of the house," Quinn objected.

"But, Quinn, it's lovely. It'll make a good background shot."

"Please don't focus on it. My neighbors were quite unhappy when I had it built. Too contemporary. They would have preferred an antebellum replica like everything else in the area, and I don't care to inflame a simmering fire at this time."

"I can't believe Quinn Robinson would give in to public pressure," Sydney taunted.

"Who gave in?" He gave her a satisfied smile. "I built it, didn't I?"

"Did you ever," she marveled, as her gaze encompassed his estate. "What if Gary filmed us while we walked around and talked? I have some questions to ask you, then we can show you fishing."

"Syd, you can be persuasive." He shrugged, realizing that it would be a subtle way to show the grounds.

They finished the questions and headed around back, where Quinn's spacious backyard included a pool, a tennis court, a small putting green, and access to a private lake.

Sydney tried to contain her sense of awe as she did her standup shot and commentary against the backdrop of the azalea-lined lake. "Now, could we get a shot of you fishing, Quinn? It would be great if we could capture you actually catching a fish out your back door."

"Hm, yes," he mumbled, and led the way down to the pier. "Takes a little luck, though."

"Well, you've certainly had your share of that."

He tried to ignore her jab. Obviously, she had no

idea of all the time, effort, and money that went into putting him where he was today.

Soon Quinn was perched in the back of his fishing boat, casting for bass, while Gary knelt on the end of the pier filming the action and Sydney posed questions and tried to hold the microphone close enough to catch his answers.

She edged closer and held the mike at arm's length. "I don't think we're picking you up, Quinn. Can you talk a little louder?"

"Sh, I see a big bass down there—" Quinn motioned and gave her a quick warning glance.

"That'd be great on camera. I'd like to get closer," Sydney said to Gary. "Do you think the cord will reach if I get in the boat with him?"

Gary eyed the space between him and where the boat was tied to the end of the pier. "Yeah, should make it."

Sydney climbed down the pier ladder and into the boat beside Quinn, stretching her mike's umbilical cord to its fullest extent. The boat tilted and rocked as she maneuvered her way to the stern.

Quinn looked back at her. "Don't tip—"

At that moment he felt a nibble on his line and instinctively jerked the fishing rod back to set the hook. The rod swung toward Sydney, who stood rather precariously balanced with one arm outstretched holding the mike.

Instinctively, she dodged. And stepped back. Right into the lake!

Her splash created waves that rocked the boat.

"Watch out!" Quinn shouted. "Man overboard!"

Gary yelled and moved quickly to gather up the

81

expensive sound equipment before it could follow Sydney into the lake.

Sydney thrashed around in the six-foot depth and quickly bobbed to the surface. Quinn had removed his shoes and was poised to jump after her, when he realized she was safe, just soaking wet. Her hair parted in the middle of her head and dripped like a blob of seaweed. The two men gaped at her, trying to hold back their laughter.

"You okay, Sydney?" Quinn asked tenderly. "Can you swim?"

She nodded. "I'm all right. I can't believe I did this!"

"Don't worry about the mike," Gary volunteered from his safe haven on the dock. "I grabbed it before it went under."

"Oh, great!" she sputtered, treading water. "I was really worried about the stupid mike. I just hope you didn't get this act on tape."

Gary didn't answer. He didn't dare.

Quinn propped one foot on the edge of the boat and rested his elbow on his knee. "Find any fish down there, Syd?"

"Very funny! Are you two going to stand there all day, or are you going to help me out of this ice bath?"

"I thought you got warm and decided to cool off by going swimming," Quinn drawled with a smile and extended his hand to her.

"You must think I'm a clumsy oaf." Sydney gratefully grabbed his hand and crawled clumsily into the boat. "Look at me! Soaking wet! And a mess!"

Quinn bit his lip and grinned. Her hair hung in limp ribbons and her blouse clung to her bodice, outlining firm breasts and narrow ribs; her slacks hugged slender hips and thighs. She looked funny and sensuous at the same time.

But Sydney's sense of humor had been doused.

Gary gazed down at Sydney, then looked at Quinn. When the two men realized she wasn't hurt and was now safely beside them on the dock, they started laughing. They slapped their thighs and hooted while Sydney steamed, arms folded across her heaving breasts.

"I'm glad I could provide such amusing entertainment for you two. Look at me. I've probably ruined my new slacks in this dirty lake!"

"Sorry, Syd," Quinn mumbled between guffaws. "It's just that you did it so easily."

"And you were quick," Gary added. "One minute you were in the boat, feeding him questions; the next, in the water! Splat!"

"Good form, though," Quinn nodded.

"You did a perfect belly flop," Gary chuckled.

"Oh! To hell with both of you!" Sydney shook her fist and scrambled to the bow of the boat and up the pier ladder. "I've ruined my clothes, I'm chilled to the bone, and all you two jerks can do is laugh at me!" Taking long strides, she started down the pier, not really knowing where she was going. Not really caring.

Quinn hurried after her and grabbed her wet arm. "Hey, you are cold. We didn't mean to offend you. Honest, Syd. Let me fix you up. Come on in the house and I'll—"

She gave him a defiant look, her green eyes flashing. "Thanks for your hospitality, but I have a job. Some people have to work, you know! Gary and I have to get back to the station so this footage can be edited for tonight's news."

"You can't go all the way into town like that," Quinn said. "Let Gary take the film back, and I'll dry your clothes and take you back later."

She paused. It did make sense. But he made her so mad, laughing at her clumsiness.

"It won't take any time to dry your clothes in the house here. And I'll feel much better about the whole thing."

"Well," she hedged slowly, thinking it would be wonderful to be dry at this moment. "Maybe you're right. He can take this stuff back. Does that sound okay to you, Gary? Quinn has offered to dry my clothes."

The burly cameraman reached them, hauling the equipment with huge, muscular arms. "Yeah, sure, Sydney."

"You're sure you don't mind?" She turned to Quinn.

"Of course not. Couldn't have planned it better myself." He gave her a sly grin, and his blue eyes twinkled. "I do feel bad about this, though."

Gary walked back to the house with Quinn and Sydney. "Be sure to watch the news tonight." Then, with a wave, he was gone.

Sydney looked at the house and wondered briefly if she had made a mistake in agreeing to do this. But she started to shiver, and she knew she had to get out of her wet clothes. "Quinn, I'm sorry for that low remark about your job. I didn't mean for it to sound that way."

"You're right, you know. I don't work, and sometimes I forget about the demands of people who do."

"But it isn't up to me to remind you. That was insensitive of me."

"It would be insensitive of me to ignore your condition. Come on," Quinn said, draping his arm around her wet shoulder. "Let's take care of you before you get chilled."

He led her into the house and through a winding hall to an immaculate bedroom with its own bath. "You can take a warm shower here. Let me see if I can find you something warm to wear until we get your clothes dry." He disappeared and in a few minutes returned with a large plaid flannel shirt. "This hunting shirt should do for now. It'll keep you warm."

"It'll be fine. Thanks." Sydney was somewhat apprehensive about being there alone with Quinn. Not that she was afraid of him; she was just unsure of her own ability to resist his strong masculine appeal, which drew her irresistibly. And also unsure of his ability to quell his desire. She could see it in his eyes when he looked at her. There was a special glow, an unspoken gleam that said, "I want you." And she was afraid that her answering gaze said, "Me, too."

"You'd better get out of those wet clothes. I'll fix us something to drink. How does coffee sound?"

She nodded silently and watched him go, almost wishing he would turn around and take her in his arms. She walked into the tiled bathroom and started to peel off her soggy clothes. When she peered at her reflection in the wall-to-wall mirror, she could understand why he'd been reluctant. She looked like a drowned rat!

Sydney soaked up the warm shower like a sponge, shampooed her hair, and even dried it with the small hand dryer. The place was well-equipped for a woman: mild deodorant, talcum powder and cologne to match, even some lovely body lotion. She emerged smelling and feeling better. The shirt came to her thighs, but it was soft and warm.

Quinn met her in the kitchen and took the bundle of wet clothes from her, silently tossing them into the washer. "This shouldn't take long. Meanwhile, how about a little coffee? You take cream, right?"

"Yes, thanks." *You remembered.* She smiled at him, then gratefully sipped from the steaming mug he offered.

Quinn's arm slipped easily around her shoulder, and he steered her into a lovely room overlooking the lake. She wanted to ask him about the bedroom she'd used. It was ready for a woman. But he mentioned it first.

"Did you find everything you needed?"

"Everything a woman could want."

"It isn't what you think, Sydney."

"What do I think?"

"That I have other women who use that room."

"You're going to tell me you don't?"

"I'm not going to tell you I haven't had other women. I have, occasionally. But that room is used by guests, not by my lover. My lover belongs in my room. In my bed. That's where I want you, Sydney."

"Where all the others have been?" She twisted out of his arms. "That's not my style, Quinn. I can't go to bed with a man just because he wants me to. Or because I find him attractive."

"Do you want to, Syd? Or am I reading the signals wrong?"

Darn it, I've never been very good at hiding my feelings. She walked to the window and sipped her coffee. The afternoon sun was dipping low over the lake, creating a glittering reddish path across its surface. "I'd have to be a fool not to. You're very appealing, Quinn. But don't you understand? I don't live that way. I've never had a lover. I have a son. We're a family, just the two of us. And I can't . . . well, I just can't."

"Can't what, Syd?" He stood beside her, one hand circling her waist, the other taking the coffee cup and setting it aside. Gently, persuasively, he pulled her against him. His fingers cupped her face, spreading sensuously over her chin and cheek and tilting her toward him. "Can't give in to feelings? To passions? You're an adult, Syd. Adults have feelings that don't go away."

He lowered his lips to hers, kissing them, caressing them in a way that made it impossible for her to resist. She melted against him, allowed herself to feel, to enjoy, to lean against a man for the first time in over a year. She wanted to give in to him, to free up her feelings, to relinquish her reserve just this once.

Sydney felt strong passion well up inside, passion that she had denied too long, passion that now gripped her and held her prisoner, taunting her every muscle. A quiver ran through her, and she let her lips part for his tongue's invasion. At first, his tongue teased the soft edges of her lips. Then slowly, erotically, it probed the warm honey of her mouth. She responded to the eventual rhythm as he plunged in and out, in and out, until she moaned softly and pressed her hips against his hard body.

He seemed to encompass her with desired warmth and needed strength. For someone as vulnerable as Sydney, it was easy to sink into Quinn Robinson's arms, to seek his masculinity.

"Oh God, Syd. I want you. I want to love you, to feel you respond to me."

"Quinn, I can't."

"But you *are.*" His hand slid down the shirt, rubbing hard against her nipples, then up again as they grew firm. "See? You want me, too."

"I don't deny that. But I can't let this happen."

"Why? Every woman has needs. Let me satisfy yours." His voice was low and persuasive as he led her to a nearby sofa.

They sank onto the sumptuous pillows, and his fingers trailed her thighs, reaching farther and farther up beneath the oversize shirt. He tenderly let his fingers touch her most sensitive spot, and she trembled with the desire that ran rampant through her. But he didn't stop. His hand moved flat along her belly, her waist, her breasts. He gently caressed her breast, squeezing it, pinching the nipple to aroused perfection, then moving to the other breast, until both were passion-swollen and aching. She thrust them forward to enhance each touch.

"Oh, Quinn—"

"Sydney, how long has it been since you've made love? Since someone's made love to you?"

"Too long, Quinn. Long before Daniel and I parted. But that doesn't mean I can merely fall—"

"Just relax, Syd. Let me make you feel like a woman again."

"You do, Quinn. Sometimes just by the way you look at me. You make me melt inside."

"I want to offer you more. Your body is full of desire, Syd. Let me make love to you." He didn't give her a chance to answer or refuse his sensuous offer. His lips covered hers, and he kissed her hard. His lips possessed hers, just as his hands owned her body.

As Quinn's exploring fingers continued their sensuous trail over her softness, Sydney felt herself giving in to him. Her breasts filled his palms to overflowing, and she pressed the taut-nippled peaks into them, writhing with the pleasure. When he framed her waist and hips with both hands, she moved in a natural, undulating motion. When his hand cupped her warm femininity, she thrust against him with a drive and force that told him of her desire.

Obeying the beseeching of her body, he touched the part of her that had been untouched for so long; he drew sensuous circles in the softness until she cried out. Her frenzy became strong and intense, and he held her firmly, bringing her to a point of overwhelming excitement.

Feverishly, she moved against him, unable to stop herself. She was unable to think of anything but the raging passion gripping her, of Quinn's ability to bring her to the brink of feeling and emotion.

Freedom, the summit, the ultimate release of feelings, brought a lusty cry to her lips. And she fell against him, collapsing. Then she lay very still.

He drew her into his arms and held her tightly, lovingly. They lay that way for a long time.

Eventually, she stirred. "Quinn, I can't believe this. I've never known that a man could be so unselfish."

"Sh, don't say anything. It's okay."

She squeezed her eyes shut. "But I've never done anything like this before."

"You've never let yourself be free. You've got to admit it was good."

She buried her face against his shoulder. "It was wonderful. But you—" She halted, embarrassed. She was the one satisfied, not him.

"I wanted you to feel that, Syd. Wanted you to know that I'm not the selfish womanizer you think I am."

She lifted her face and looked at him honestly. "You are not at all what I expected, Quinn Robinson. You aren't even who I thought you were. Every time I'm with you, I discover you're someone different from my original concept. I thought I knew you. But I didn't."

"Sydney, beautiful Sydney, don't build me into someone I'm not. I'm a man who wants you very much. I won't hide that. But I wanted to touch you, to feel your response, to know your feelings. And I want you to know mine."

She nodded. It was only fair.

But he shifted and kissed her temple. "Not now. Later. I think your clothes are finished washing. We need to dry them."

Once again, she was surprised. She shook her head and framed his face with her hands. "Quinn, you're funny. And amazing."

"I'll get your clothes. You stay put." He kissed her quickly.

90

She smiled into his gorgeous blue eyes. "I am a little weak."

"I'll warm up our coffee, too." He chuckled as he left the room.

Sydney lay back on a sofa pillow and hugged her arms, suddenly feeling cold and empty without Quinn. He was a remarkable man who made her feel alive—like a woman again. She smiled to herself as she thought of him, of how he'd lifted her spirits and brought joy to her life the few times she'd been with him. How he played with the kids in the park that day with the enthusiasm of a clown. How he helped her, gave her interviews when he'd rather not. How he'd made love to her and neither of them had completely undressed.

Now what would he expect from her? Everything she had to give? She wasn't entirely opposed to the idea.

But when he returned, humming, he brought fresh coffee and made no indication that he expected anything of her. He handed her the steaming mug and waited until she sat upright. Then he joined her on the sofa. "Your clothes should be dry in another thirty minutes, Syd."

"Thank you for taking care of them." *Of me,* she wanted to add. She noticed how steady his hands were, how large and secure. How she liked those hands! And she couldn't help remembering how they felt caressing her, how warm and wonderful they made her feel.

She attempted to divert the conversation. "I'm glad I had the opportunity to meet your girls. How are they?"

"Fine. They're back with Stacey and will stay there until school's out. Then they'll probably be here with me for most of the summer."

"I'll bet they love it here. It's a child's perfect fantasy. Everything for a kid to do. Swimming. Tennis. Fishing. Boating. Even golf." She laughed, but she noticed that Quinn didn't join her. "Quinn? Did you hear me?"

Suddenly, he looked different, as if her mentioning the girls had triggered something. His face had grown tense, resigned. "Yeah, yeah, you're right. They can do anything they want to. Benefits of being Quinn Robinson's kids."

"Quinn, what's wrong? All of a sudden, you seem . . . bitter. You never sounded that way before. At least, I didn't notice it."

He stood up and walked to the window. "It isn't bitterness, Syd. It's—oh, hell."

"If it's personal, I didn't mean to—"

"No. It isn't."

"The girls are all right, aren't they?"

"Yeah, fine."

"Quinn, they're really great kids. I want you to know how much Chad enjoyed playing with them. And he loves the kite they gave him. You know, they are very generous children. A lot like their dad."

"Yeah, they're generous, all right. To a fault."

"So what's wrong?"

"Nothing."

"Quinn . . ."

He sighed and spoke finally in a strained voice. "Remember Lindi asked to buy a balloon for her sick friend?"

"Yes, I thought that was very nice."

"Well, we went by the hospital to deliver it. I expected some kid who was having her tonsils removed, or something equally minor." He paused and uttered a hollow laugh. "You know what's wrong with Beth? The kid's got *leukemia.* Imagine my surprise when Lindi said, 'Come on, Daddy, meet Beth. She's got leukemia!' as if it were a bad cold."

"Oh Quinn, how awful!"

"Sydney, it's tragic! Do you know what that means? We're talking about a disease that's terminal. But the girls stayed and played with her, just as if she were normal."

"Good for them. How is she?"

"Well, she's in the hospital for more treatment and I think she's doing better. She's in remission and responding to treatment, but—"

"Yes?"

"She's bald, Syd." He turned around with a strange expression on his face. "Have you ever seen a kid with no hair? A little girl? The chemotherapy does that to them. Every kid on the floor was bald!"

"I'm sure the contrast with your girls was stark." Sydney walked over to him. "It sounds like you had more trouble adjusting to Beth's appearance than your children did, Quinn."

He nodded slowly. "Y'know, you're right. I had a helluva time with that. I kept looking at her, remembering how she played around here last Easter vacation. And how sick she is now. It struck her so fast. To be perfectly honest, I couldn't wait to leave."

"I'll bet your visit and bringing the girls to play made Beth very happy."

"Yeah, her mother thanked us over and over. Beth's family lives on the other side of the lake. The girls play together whenever they're here with me. They took horseback riding lessons and went to summer camp together last year. It was so hard looking Beth's mother in the face. I almost felt guilty because my kids are healthy. Isn't that crazy?"

"No, Quinn, it's normal."

"Oh Syd, do you know how lucky we are to have healthy kids?"

"Yes. But it doesn't hurt to be reminded once in a while." She wrapped her arms around him and pressed him to her, returning some of the warm comfort he had given her.

Quinn folded his arms around her and held her tightly. "Yes, we're very lucky, Syd."

She smiled and pressed a kiss to his chest. "The evening news should be on soon. Want to see how a lucky man spends his day? Before an unlucky reporter falls into the lake and he has to wash her clothes!"

CHAPTER SIX

"My first on-camera story. I'm so nervous. Everything could hinge on this." Sydney sat at the edge of her seat and stared at the blank TV screen.

"Everything? I didn't realize how important it was to you. I'd have mowed the grass." Quinn moved distractedly to switch on the TV.

"Oh yes," Sydney breathed. "My boss will probably use this interview to determine whether I stay in front of the camera or work in the back room. It's very important to me."

Quinn heaved himself into a nearby chair and tugged on his lower lip. Obviously, his thoughts were elsewhere.

Sydney sat nervously glued to the tube throughout the newscast.

Finally the sports news closed, and Sydney's segment began with a montage of Quinn's career highlights. Then, in a voice-over, Sydney listed his accomplishments, all achieved before he was thirty. Framed by a magnificent backdrop of the azalea-lined lake, Sydney stated that they would discover what Quinn Robinson was doing today at home in Tallahassee.

Sydney glanced at Quinn with a quick, nervous smile.

Quinn perked up at shots of him directing the bird dogs, a few seconds of his hour-long golf workshop, then the walking interview with his beautiful contemporary house subtly in the background.

Quinn gestured futilely. "It's almost over! All that time, all those years of work, condensed into mere seconds! It even took you all day to film it."

" 'Fraid so," Sydney nodded succinctly. "A whole day's work, condensed to a three-minute shot."

Quinn watched glumly. "Years . . . years of playing. And now what?"

The piece ran about as long as Sydney had expected. All things considered, she was pleased. After all, it was her first story. If she was a little nervous, well, that was to be expected.

As the end approached, Quinn laughed at the shot of him casting for fish. "You can't even tell it was staged with the bass boat tied right to the end of the pier."

Sydney nodded and hoped Lee had the tape clipped at the right spot. She would die if—"*Oh no!*" She bolted from her chair and shrieked in horror. There in living color was Sydney belly-flopping into the glistening lake!

That one moment on film had doused her budding career.

"Oh no! How could they make such a mistake?" She moved anxiously around the room, wailing and wringing her hands. "How could they do this to me? Oh, damn, damn! How could Lee let this happen?"

Quinn ignored her laments. "My whole life, reduced

to a few minutes' worth of film clips. Now all I'm doing is playing."

Sydney ran her hands through her hair. "Mr. Reinhardt will never hire me after this. Never! I looked like a fool."

"Running the dogs, fishing, playing golf and tennis, playing with the kids—"

"What?" Sydney whirled on him. "Quinn, what *are* you talking about?"

"Do you realize that all I do is *play?* The most serious accomplishment in my life these days is to teach someone else to play golf." He looked wildly at her. "To teach *someone else* how to play!"

"So? What's wrong with that?"

He stood and gestured toward her. "I'll tell you what's wrong. I'm skimming through life living frivolously."

"You're having fun, Quinn. You can afford to."

"But, life is—must be—more than that."

Sydney gave him an impatient look. "Peggy Lee used to sing a song about the subject. *Is That All There Is?* It skimmed over everything important in life."

"That's me. Aimless. Doing nothing substantial."

"Oh, Quinn, that's ridiculous. You're taking care of your kids, and you're doing what you want to do. You don't have to answer to anyone but yourself. Everybody envies you your position. Do you know how lucky you are?"

"Well, I can tell you now, I'm dissatisfied with what I see! An empty hull of a man."

"You make me sick, Quinn Robinson!" Sydney surprised Quinn—and herself—with her outburst. But she continued, unable to stop herself. "You have everything in the world you want! Money. Beautiful kids. Big house, pool, lake. You don't have to worry about a job. Do you know what happened to me today? Do you even care? I'm ruined! Before I can even get started, my career is down the drain. Literally, in your stupid lake!"

"What the hell do you mean, Sydney?"

"Are you blind? Didn't you see what happened to me? Haven't you heard a word I've said?"

"I heard you say I'm a man who plays a lot. And you're right. My whole life has been—"

"I'm not talking about your past. I'm talking about my future. And my son's future. Now it looks so bleak!"

"Because of that one little incident? One interview can't make or break you, Syd."

"Oh no? Well, when it's all you have to show, it can. And when that one shot is of me doing a belly-flop in the lake!"

He brightened. "Well, at least they didn't show you climbing back into the boat looking like a—"

"Drowned rat?"

"I would have said drenched mermaid." He shrugged with a grin. "But you weren't exactly graceful. Be thankful for small favors."

"Thankful? For something that ruined my career? You are so narrow-minded, Quinn Robinson. You don't know what it's like to work a day in your life! And you can't relate to those of us who do! I'm ready to go home. Where's my purse?"

"Out in the Florida room."

"On second thought, I don't want to go home. Take me to the television station. That's where I left my car.

I'm going to give Lee a piece of my mind! I thought he was my friend." She stormed out of the house, still fuming.

Preoccupied with his own thoughts, Quinn drove her back to town in stormy silence.

"I tell you, Lora, my whole career flashed before my eyes! Bleak, that's what it is. Oh, I should never have fooled with Quinn Robinson in the first place. How could I have been so stupid as to think he would help me get anywhere?"

"He helped you cinch an A in Interviewing."

Sydney whirled around. "He had an ulterior motive in mind. *Me!*"

"Syd, aren't you being a little melodramatic?"

"How can you say that, Lora, when you know how much is at stake here?"

"You got the job, didn't you?"

"Not *the* job. *A* job. The lowest of the low, except for my old gofer position."

"Settle down and tell me about it. What did Reinhardt say?"

Sydney flung herself onto a stool in Lora's kitchen and took a sip of the wine Lora had just poured. "He was there, working late, and he motioned me into his office. Said he'd noticed me, been keeping his eye on me around the station. That he knew what good work I could do, given the right position."

Lora tossed her hair. "I think he's the one with the ulterior motive. You'd better watch out for that guy, Syd."

"Oh, no, Lora. He's very sincere."

"And very handsome, if I remember correctly."

Sydney shook her head stubbornly. "Fortunately, he didn't refer to my tumble in the lake, but I'm sure he saw it. Do you know how embarrassing that is to a reporter? He said my reporting needed some work. And he'd give me a chance to learn some skills and get some on-camera experience. Now I get to report on local sports, like high-school stuff."

"Well, Syd, that's better than nothing. He did give you another chance."

"I know, but it isn't what I wanted. What I *need.*"

"Sydney, sweetheart, didn't they teach you in college that you don't start at the top in any field, especially the one you choose? I'd say television is one of the hardest in which a female can achieve success."

"Oh boy, are you ever right about that! It's a male-dominated field."

"And you picked a particularly tough area. Sports. That's still quite male-dominated."

"Yeah, I know." Sydney ran a finger around the glass rim. "I was so furious when I talked to Lee tonight. He said it was Margarite's idea to show my flop in the lake, and he couldn't do anything about it. She thought it'd be cute. Well, 'cute' almost cost me my job, and she probably knew it would. For sure, it kept me at the bottom of the barrel."

"That's exactly what she wanted, sweetheart. Better watch out for her, too. Sounds as though she wields a lot of power at that station."

Sydney shook her head. "Does she ever. Wouldn't I love to see her perfect blond hair dripping wet! I'd like to tell her off, but I don't dare. I hate this! I hate being at the bottom! I've been there so long."

"Take it easy, Syd. Tell me about your day with

100

Quinn. Now, talk about handsome. That man has real sex appeal."

"Lora! He's just some rich guy who can't see past his pool and tennis court and lake. He thinks everyone lives like he does. Like a king."

"Wait a minute." Lora held her hand up. "Is this the same guy who saved you when you needed a special interview for class? And understood your situation as a single parent better than anyone? And listened to you when you needed him? And took those kids under his wing in the park and everyone had a wonderful day, including you? And has the most devastating blue eyes in the world?"

Sydney stormed around the room. "He's the one who is blind to those who work for a living. He's narrow-minded. And he can't think of anyone but himself. He's the one who wants—"

"Please, don't destroy my fantasy of this guy. I thought he was nearly perfect."

"Perfect? Ha!"

"Well, go ahead and finish. What does he want?" Lora leaned on the counter toward Sydney, a fiendish gleam in her eyes. "You, yes?"

"He wants his way!"

"Did he get it?" Lora's eyes danced.

Sydney gulped her wine and pushed her empty glass across the table. "I've got to get busy. Chad? Ready to go?" she called.

"Wait, Syd." Lora followed her to the door. "Forget his way. What about yours?"

"There's more to life than *that,* Lora."

"Oh yeah? What? Money? He fills that bill nicely, too."

Sydney folded her arms and leaned against the doorframe. "What about love, Lora?"

"Wake up, Syd. We both tried that the first time. And see where it got us?"

Sydney tossed up her hands. "Maybe you're right. What should I go after? Money or sex?"

"Money, definitely," Lora answered readily. "You can always get sex."

"Lora, you're awful!" Syd giggled and opened the door. "If I ever took you seriously, I'd be in big trouble."

"I'm serious!" Lora claimed. "Go after the money, sweetheart."

"Well, sex is all Quinn's offering."

"On second thought, maybe you'd better take it."

Sydney shook her head as Chad appeared from another room. Together they crossed the hall to their apartment.

First thing the next morning, balloons arrived at Sydney's door. A bouquet of them, tied with a big red ribbon. Each carried a message: BALLOON OF MY HEART; LIFE IS JUST A BUNCH OF BALLOONS; YOU'RE THE WIND BENEATH MY BALLOON; A BALLOON IS A ROUND MIRACLE; SMILE, YOU'RE ON CANDID BALLOON; YOU BALLOON UP MY LIFE.

"Wow, Mom!" Chad exclaimed, reaching up with both hands. "Floaty balloons! Who sent 'em?"

"Only one person that I can think of would do anything this crazy." She grabbed the card as Chad whisked the balloons away.

"What fun! Uh-oh, one escaped to the ceiling, Mom. I'll climb up and get it."

Sydney opened the card and started to smile before she read his scrawl. *Balloons are perfect. I'm not. And I do care. Quinn.*

Her smile spread, and she pressed the card to her pounding heart. She felt like a teen-ager with a crush. Giddy and happy. Her first thought was to call him, but before she had a chance, the phone rang. *It might be him!* She lunged for the receiver but her smile faded quickly. It wasn't Quinn.

"Daniel? . . . You what? You want him this week-end? . . . Not overnight . . . I know you have rights, but . . . yes . . . yes." Weakly, she hung up.

The rest of her day was a mess as she tried to get Chad organized to spend the night with his father. Although Sydney was an emotional wreck, she hid it from her son. After all, Daniel did have a right to spend some time with Chad. And their son deserved more than an occasional weekend father. But why did he have to start now? She just wasn't prepared, physically or emotionally. That night she called Lora.

"Sorry, Sydney. I don't have time to talk. I've got a date. With a college prof! Tell you all about him tomorrow."

"But, Lora, I need—"

"Syd, I'm late now."

"Okay, have a good time, Lora." She dropped the phone into its cradle. Her eyes rested on the card that had arrived this morning with the balloons. In the melee, she'd forgotten about them. *About him.* She suddenly remembered his words. *I do care.*

She picked up the phone again and punched the numbers slowly. "Quinn?"

"Syd! What's up?"

"Oh, Quinn." She chuckled in spite of her sagging spirits. "Balloons, of course."

"Syd, you all right? What's wrong, honey?"

"I'm—" She choked, unable to finish.

"Want to talk about it?"

"Yes."

"I'll be right there."

Quinn arrived within the hour with a smile and a bottle of expensive wine.

"Just what I needed," Sydney admitted.

"Me? Or the wine?"

"You," she whispered, drawing him inside the apartment.

His midnight blue eyes looked deeply into hers for a second before his lips claimed hers. She was soft and receptive and seemed to absorb his warmth and energy.

He lifted his head, but they remained close. "I thought about you all day."

"Thanks for the balloons. They were wonderful."

"I was a jerk yesterday. Please believe I do care, Syd. Did you lose your job?"

She shook her head. "No."

"See? They can't function without you. And I'm finding it increasingly difficult."

"Quinn—"

He looked over her shoulder. "Where's the kid?"

She pushed herself away from Quinn's warm protection. "With his father."

"Oh. Is that what's wrong?"

"Well, it's not as if this happens every other weekend. This is only the third time in the last six months he's even wanted to see Chad. And it's the first time he's taken him for the whole night."

"I see."

"Quinn, I know you think I'm crazy. Broken families do this all the time."

"But you don't."

She breathed a sigh. "Right. I'm sure I'll get used to it, *if* Daniel ever does this again."

"He probably will when he finds out what a neat kid Chad is."

She nodded glumly.

"Do you have a corkscrew? The occasion seems to call for a little *vino.*" He followed her into the tiny kitchen. He halted before her wall phone and read aloud the sign posted above it: THE GRAIN OF SAND IN THE OYSTER IS THE IRRITANT THAT MAKES THE PEARL. Is that what drives you on, Syd?"

She smiled secretly. "Daniel is my irritant. And I intend to make a pearl of my life in spite of him." She dug out a corkscrew and two wineglasses.

"You are one determined lady." He gave her an admiring glance before tackling his project.

Sydney watched Quinn's strong hands as he gripped the wine bottle and twisted the metal coil into the cork. With precision, he slowly pulled the cork out, then held the mouth of the bottle near his nose. "Ah, nice." He splashed a small amount of the pale liquid into a glass and presented it to her. "Madam."

She inhaled appreciatively, then sipped. "Very nice."

"Chenin Blanc, semidry," he said, pouring the glasses full with a comic flair.

They toasted, both realizing when their eyes met

what might come of the evening. Daringly, they drank anyway. Maybe it was time to free up their emotions. They sat in the tiny apartment living room.

It was a far cry from Quinn's spacious house, where every room was graced with a lovely view. Here there were no views, no expensive furniture, nothing fancy. Just the two of them, caring, trying to understand. Not resisting the inevitable course of nature that tugged at them.

"It isn't that I mind Daniel taking Chad," Sydney finally admitted. "After all, he is his father. But why now? Chad hardly knows him. And Daniel barely knows his own son."

"Some men feel uncomfortable when their children are very young. Now that Chad is older, maybe Daniel feels more at ease."

"Humph! He felt comfortable enough to bring along his blond friend!"

"Ah, therein lies the problem," Quinn deducted.

"I'm not jealous, if that's what you're thinking," she said sternly.

"Sure, sure." Quinn's hand crept around her neck, digging beneath her mass of auburn hair.

"Okay, I'll admit it. I'm angry!"

"Do you care?"

"That he has another woman? Not now. I'm used to it. He left me for another woman. That's when I vowed I'd show him I could make it without him."

"Aha! Revenge!"

"Damn right. And I'll show him someday." She paused to sip the delicious wine. "It just infuriates me that he would bring that woman around Chad. They aren't even married."

"Sydney, you're not going to lose Chad's affection. You are his mother. And no one will replace you in his heart."

She blinked back tears and pressed her forehead to his shoulder. With Quinn's arms around her, she felt warm and secure. "Thank you, Quinn. You always say just what I need to hear."

He lifted her chin with one finger. "You know what you need tonight?"

She grinned. "Number one proposition?"

He shook his head. "Advance to propositions two and three. I'll bet you haven't eaten. I know a place that serves the best barbecue this side of the Suwannee. And they have a bluegrass band that plays the liveliest foot-stompin' music you've ever heard."

She threw back her head and laughed. "Sounds great. You are exactly what I need tonight, Quinn Robinson."

His eyes settled on her, grateful for her smile, hoping her words were true. Never had he wanted so strongly to be everything a woman needed. And never had he desired a woman so badly yet refrained from taking her to bed.

Zestfully, they ate barbecue and drank beer and shuffled across the wood-shaving-covered dance floor until they were exhausted. It was after midnight before they returned.

"Want to come in for a nightcap? I have a bottle of some wonderfully expensive wine to finish." Sydney pulled him inside the door and pressed her hands against his chest. "I don't know when I've *ever* had so much fun, Quinn."

"Entirely my pleasure, Syd." He framed her face

107

and kissed her tenderly, letting his thumbs caress her cheeks.

She returned the kiss. "Quinn, about proposition number one—"

He pressed her lips with a single finger. "I'd like to rename proposition number one proposal number one. My proposal, Sydney Jacques, is that we make love, mutually." He kissed her again.

She closed her eyes. "Mmm . . . yes."

"Yes? Did you say—"

She took his hand and pressed it to her heart, to her breast. He felt the warm throbbing beneath the soft plumpness.

"Yes." Her answer was firm, and she led him down the hall past Chad's bedroom to hers.

They undressed in the dark, quietly. And when he turned to face her, Sydney gasped involuntarily to see him so aroused by her.

"You haven't changed your mind, have you?" His voice was low and gravelly. "Don't do this to me, Syd."

"Oh, Quinn, it's just that you're so—so beautiful." A ripple of anticipation coursed through her limbs. It had been a long time since she'd seen a nude man, a man boldly eager for her.

He moved closer and took her hand. "Touch me, Syd. I want you to know every inch of me, just as I want to know you." His voice faltered as her fingers reached him. "I won't hurt you."

Tentatively, she stroked his heated chest, his taut belly, his turgid flesh. "Quinn, I—I've never been with another man besides my husband."

Quinn pulled her into his arms and buried his face

in her wealth of hair. His hands spread across her smooth back, crushing her breasts to his chest, thrusting his hardened body against her.

"Sydney, I can hardly wait for you. I've wanted you so long."

"Me, too," she admitted softly.

He pushed her back and let his eyes, then his fingertips, feast on her entire length. With a low rumble deep in his chest, he bent to taste every bit of her.

She breathed his name through parted lips as his kisses traversed down her quivering body. His mouth closed over her nipples, drawing each to the size and color of a pouting raspberry. His tongue outlined the prominent beaded circles, then drew a moist line down the throbbing valley between her breasts. She arched her small body and began to ache for the satisfaction only he could give.

Warm, wet kisses were scattered over her silken belly, reaching lower and lower.

She gripped his shoulders with sudden ferocity. "Make love to me, Quinn."

He lowered her to the bed. "Oh, my love, you're so beautiful, so very beautiful." His curious fingertips caressed her everywhere, touched and probed, teased and taunted until she thought she'd go crazy with the sweet torment.

Her arms, once tentative, pulled him to her with a desperate hunger. "Quinn—"

Gently but firmly, he parted her thighs. "Syd, are you ready for me?"

"Oh yes. I want you, Quinn. Now!"

He hovered over her and lowered for a long, deliberate kiss as he settled slowly on top of her.

Sydney hooked her legs around him and arched toward him. "Oh hurry, Quinn!"

"Take it easy, honey. It's been a long time for you." He lifted her hips and gently moved into her. "I don't want to hurt you."

"You won't." She raised herself toward him, trying to speed him. But he continued his agonizingly slow entry, each moment increasing the pressure building between them.

Finally he let himself be completely captured by her. She smiled up at him. "Oh God, Quinn. I never knew it would be like this."

"You all right?" He began an exquisite stroking motion that brought her to an unbearable state of passion.

"Yes—yes!"

She moved with him, certain that she had never been loved quite like this. He made her feel such a high degree of emotion and sensuality that the two became entwined into a spiral of passion that gripped her, threatening not to let go. And Sydney never wanted it to end.

Higher and higher they spiraled. When they reached the summit, he became frenzied and uncontrolled. "Ah, Syd . . . my love . . . my love!"

She accepted all he had to offer, reaching her own peak with a wildness never before experienced. Later, she wondered if he remembered what he'd said. And if he meant it.

They lay wrapped together all night. Quinn held her to him, possessively, and he knew he wanted her forever, knew he never wanted another man to make love to her. He had to have her all to himself. But he couldn't tell her that. He could only express his affection toward her by possessing her physically. And so he did, later on in the middle of the night.

And Sydney received him with open arms.

CHAPTER SEVEN

"Lee, I know what you're going to say, but it's unfair! Give me another chance. I swear I'll do better next time."

"Hell, if we give you another chance, you might break a bone. Or kill yourself. On camera, yet!"

"No! No, I won't! I'll be very careful. Can I help it if I'm a little clumsy?"

"A *little?* You're an accident waiting to happen! A walking lawsuit for the station. Sit down, Sydney." Lee moved slowly to his office door and closed it, then ambled back around to his desk.

Sydney listened to his deliberate footsteps on the floor tile with a feeling of impending doom. But she launched her defense anyway. "You just threw me out there with no guidance. No experience. No training. What do I know about wrestling?"

Lee shook his head. "Obviously, nothing."

"I'll learn. I promise. Just let me have another crack at it."

Lee winced at her choice of words and shook his head. "I'm sending Bradford out today to cover. We can't afford another screwup. This wrestling clinic has wrestlers and coaches from all over the state. It's very important to cover it adequately. And fairly."

"If it's the shiner, I have an idea. How about an eyepatch? A reporter with a pink patch. It might become popular, might even boost ratings!"

Lee rolled his eyes.

Sydney continued frantically. "Lee, I couldn't help it if those heavyweights scooted outside their circle. They're supposed to stay inside that circle, aren't they?"

"If you knew anything about the sport, you'd know they use the out-of-bounds area to maneuver their opponent."

"Well, it's certainly different from the wrestling I've seen on TV."

"Different? Sydney, it's not even the same game!"

"Their feet just got tangled with mine. Look, I won't stand there again to do my lead-in. Oh, Lee—"

"Shut up, Sydney. I'm reassigning you. We've never had so many irate calls from the public. You're just lucky Reinhardt likes you. I've seen him fire better reporters than you for less."

"I thought you were on my side, Lee."

"I'm trying, Sydney, but you're working against me. Look at you! You almost got yourself killed by that two-hundred-and-fifty-pound wrestler!" He sighed helplessly. "Now, I want you to help Dixie with community affairs."

"Community what?"

"You even have a title. Assistant community affairs director. Same salary. Be thankful you still have a job. Now, get out. Go put a steak or something on that shiner."

Sydney sulked out of Lee's office and headed home. What a day for this to happen. She'd be graduating tonight, and already the job of her dreams was rapidly slipping through her fingers. The eye wasn't so bad, just a little bruised. It would go away in a couple of days. Lee had just overreacted. And now she was stuck with this nothing job! Community affairs, indeed! How could her private life with Quinn be so wonderful and her career be falling apart?

"Can I help you with anything?" Lora leaned on the bedroom door and watched Sydney scamper around the room, throwing on clothes.

"What a way to celebrate my graduation! Demoted!"

"They didn't cut your salary, did they?"

Sydney shook her head. "Thank heavens Mr. Reinhardt likes me!"

"Then it isn't a demotion, just a change. I told you to watch out for that guy."

"What? He saved my skin!"

"Maybe he wants your skin!" Lora suggested. "Anyway, maybe this is for the best."

"How could it be? I'm not in front of the camera anymore. Don't you understand, Lora? That's where I want to be." Sydney sat on the edge of the bed and pulled sheer hose over each slender leg.

"Have you looked at yourself in the last twelve hours?" Lora demanded. "You look like you've been hit by a Mack truck! Not exactly the prettiest face to put before the public. Anyway, maybe it's a temporary move, until you heal."

Sydney stood up and slid the pantyhose around her

114

hips. "Nope. I have a title. Assistant community affairs director. Lee wanted to get me away from the cameras."

"Have you ever considered that you might like this better?"

Sydney gave her friend a disgusted look. "Lora, I *wanted* the weekend sportscaster's job. I had to settle for reporter. How the hell can Daniel see my success if I'm hidden in the back somewhere?"

"He'll know, Syd."

"But I wanted to *show* him. It would be so sweet, after the hell he's put me through."

Lora watched Sydney's jerky movements as she finished dressing. "Don't let this drive for revenge consume you, Syd."

"Lora, don't you think Daniel's desertion has consumed my life? And practically ruined it."

"Yes, it's been rough," Lora admitted. "But get beyond it, Syd. You're graduating. You have a good job, despite what happened today. You have Quinn—"

Sydney's head snapped up and she looked at the clock. "Quinn! He'll be here any minute!"

"Does he know about this?" Lora tapped her own eye.

"No. I didn't have a chance to tell him." Sydney called into the other room. "Chad? Are you ready?"

"Perhaps you should have warned him."

"Do I look that bad?" Sydney paused to pat more makeup onto the deep purple crescent beneath her right eye.

"Not bad"—Lora sniffed—"if you like a single multicolored eye. Personally, I think they should match."

"Chad? Would you check on him, Lora?" At the

sound of the doorbell, Sydney grabbed a brush and began to stab furiously at her hair. "He's here!"

Lora disappeared into Chad's bedroom. "How are you doing, Chad? What's that sticky stuff on your face? Oh my, what's on your shirt? Let's get cleaned up here. This is a very important night for your mommy."

Sydney dashed to the door and flung it open. She smiled breathlessly up at Quinn, forgetting about her black eye. It had been two whole days since she'd seen him, and she missed him terribly. Then she noticed the flowers he'd brought. "Roses! Oh Quinn, how beautiful! How thoughtful!"

"Congratulations, graduate! Now you're on your way to—" He halted midsentence. "What the hell happened to you? Daniel didn't do this, did he?"

"No, no." She smiled bravely, taking the flowers and pulling him inside. "Hazards of my job. Come on in. I want you to meet my best friend, Lora."

He took an unsettled breath. "For you, Syd, almost everything you touch becomes a hazard."

She kissed him quickly. "But not you, Quinn."

"Are you going to tell me how this happened?"

She inhaled the bouquet's exquisite fragrance. "I tangled with some wrestlers."

"Wrestlers?" Quinn was growing more alarmed by the second. "How?"

"Our feet got mixed up, and I fell. That's all. And the mike hit my—"

"Hit your eye! My God, Sydney! You could have broken your cheekbone! Or worse!"

"Please, Quinn. It hasn't been a great day. Do I have to get this from you, too?"

He wrapped his arms around her and pulled her to him. "No, honey, it's just that I get upset when you get hurt." His lips sought hers, kissing her cheek and nose along the way.

She leaned against him, reveling in his security, in the warm aura of his kiss. But a yell, similar in tone to the one Tarzan used in the jungle, interrupted the sweet moment.

"Waaaaaa-aaa, Quinn! Yeah! You're here!"

Quinn raised his head with a patient smile. Chad had somehow attached himself to Quinn's shoulders and was hugging with all his might. "Hey, old man! How're you doing?"

"Fine! I saved you a slice of pizza from my supper."

"Thanks, but I thought I'd take your mom out to a fancy dinner tonight after her graduation."

"Oh." There was clear disappointment on his little face as Quinn lowered him to the floor.

"But I'll tell you what. My girls are coming to Tallahassee this weekend, and we're going camping. How would you and your mom like to come along? We could hike and fish and row boats—"

"Yeah! I'd love it! I've never been camping!" Chad enthused.

"Never?"

"Can we go, Mom? Can we? Say yes!"

Sydney stared dubiously at Quinn. "I wish you'd mentioned this earlier so we could have discussed it privately." Her eyes dropped to Chad, and she forced a smile.

"You've never been camping either?" Quinn asked quietly.

"Sure, I went camping once when I was ten. Got

the worst case of poison ivy the emergency room doc had ever seen. It made a lasting impression on me and took the intrigue out of the whole idea of roughing it."

Quinn gave her a convincing smile. "Don't forget, we'll be staying in the motor home. It's hard to say you're roughing it when you have a blender and a trash compactor. No sleeping bags necessary. Everyone will have real beds. And I guarantee there will be no romping in the weeds."

"You're very persuasive, Quinn," she murmured with a sigh.

"Is that a yes?"

"Well, I guess—"

"Whoopee! Camping!" Chad began to dance around the room.

"It'll be a terrific way to celebrate your graduation, Sydney. Out in the great outdoors." He winked. "I'll show you how to detect those wicked poisonous leaves of ivy."

"Yes, well, all I want to do is steer clear of them." She forced a smile, thinking that camping with three kids was not her idea of a celebration. But Quinn seemed enthusiastic about it. And Chad was so wild, there was no disappointing him now.

"It'll be a cinch in the motor home."

"A cinch? If you say so . . ." Her eyes met Lora's, and silent doubts were exchanged. "Uh, I want you to meet my dear friend, Lora Jefferson. Quinn Robinson."

Lora stretched out her hand. "Hello, Quinn. I've heard so much about you. Camping sounds quite fascinating. Sydney has always thrived in the great outdoors."

Sydney cast her dearest friend in the world green-eyed daggers.

When Sydney agreed to go camping with the three kids, she forgot to include the dog. Chad immediately fell in love with Happy, the girls' rangy golden retriever. And the feeling was mutual. One lick on Chad's chin, and Happy knew he'd found a friend for life.

Before leaving town, the six of them trailed through the grocery store, piling food and bug repellent into a shopping cart. The manager caught up with them and sent the dog out. Chad objected and marched out to stand outside the door with him. "Be sure to get marshmallows," he instructed Trina. "And crunchy dog biscuits for Happy!"

By the time they reached the check-out, Sydney was sure they had enough food to feed an army for a month. At least the motor home provided food, drink, and bathrooms until they arrived at the great outdoors. Admittedly, it was nice driving straight to the lake with no pit stops.

Quinn pulled into their previously reserved camping spot, and they all tumbled out. "There it is, Sydney. Lake Seminole. Isn't it beautiful? Not exactly wilderness, but close enough this time."

"Are we in Georgia, now, Daddy?" Lindi asked.

"Yep. Red Georgia clay. Breathe that clean, country air, kids!" Quinn inhaled deeply and patted his belly.

"Me and Happy want to take a walk," Chad announced right away.

Sydney looked at the unfamiliar camping area with

its huge lake nearby. "Wait a minute, honey. You might get lost."

"Lost?" Chad scoffed. "Me 'n Happy can find our way through anything."

Quinn gave Trina a wink. "Why don't you girls go along? And stay on the path."

"Don't go far," called Sydney.

"They'll be fine," Quinn said with a reassuring pat on her arm. "Trina and Lindi have been here before. They know their way around the campground. And they know not to go too far."

Sydney smiled her relief. "Chad is in heaven, you know."

"So am I." Quinn grinned and latched the motor-home door. "Gives us a chance to be alone." He pulled her down into his arms on the small sofa and began kissing her neck.

"Quinn! Don't you think we should be doing something while they're gone?" she managed between giggles.

"Mmm, honey, we *are* doing something." He brought her shorts-clad body closer to his.

"I mean about setting up camp." The masculine force of his hairy thighs insinuated against her smoothness, tantalizing her.

"We're self-contained, honey." His lips captured hers tenderly and sweetly forced them apart. The moist probing of his tongue prompted her to open her lips. Her tongue met his in a teasing match, then allowed his further entry.

With a soft moan, she relaxed in his arms. This was her idea of a vacation, celebrating her desire for Quinn and relishing his seemingly unbounded desire for her.

120

As the kiss deepened, so did his boldness. His hands slipped beneath her T-shirt and caressed her breasts. She arched against his touch and wanted to fling aside her bra so his hands could do justice to her bare, burning skin.

He continued to kiss her neck while he turned her back to him and wedged her between his thighs. He unsnapped her bra and slid both his hands around to capture the fullness of her breasts. Clasping the nipples between his thumbs and forefingers, he squeezed gently. "Ah, Sydney, I love your breasts."

Releasing her simmering breasts, he reached down to stroke her bare thighs below her shorts. "I love your legs. They're gorgeous and straight and firm and—"

The sensitive skin on her inner thighs tingled as one hand closed over the juncture at the top of her legs. "And I love this part of you. So luscious."

A loud pounding on the motor-home door interrupted the sensuous moment.

"Daddy? Daddy! Are you in there? Come here, quick!" The child's voice sounded excited, and Quinn practically dumped Sydney onto the floor as he lunged for the door.

"What is it?" he asked as he fumbled with the lock.

"It's Happy. And Chad."

"Wha-a-at?" Sydney grabbed frantically for the loose ends of her bra and stumbled after Quinn.

Outside the camper stood Chad and the once-golden retriever, both covered with mud.

"Chad, are you all right?" But Sydney knew as his blue eyes peered out from his mud-covered face that he was.

"I see you met up with some of this wonderful red Georgia clay," Quinn commented.

"All over," Sydney breathed, marveling at how one little kid could get caked with mud so quickly. "And it probably stains, too."

"Happy's a mud dog!" Lindi giggled.

"I tried to tell Chad not to follow Happy," Trina explained in her little-mother tone.

"Did not!" Chad gave her a defiant look. "Anyway, I had to save Happy from the mud!"

"You look like Mud Man!" Lindi taunted, pointing and giggling. "Mud Man! Mud Man!"

Both girls laughed teasingly, and Chad joined the fun by raising both soggy arms monster-style. Roaring, he began walking toward them with straight legs. "Aaarrrr!"

The girls shrieked, and Happy took one look at Mud Man and started barking and jumping around.

"Watch out for Happy! He's muddy!"

"Eeeek! He got me muddy!"

"Mud Man's gonna get us!"

"Catch Happy! Don't let him run away!"

"Hold on to him!"

"Aggg, he's wet! Chad, stop it!"

Above the cacophony, Quinn's baritone blared. *"Quiet, everyone!* Have you got the dog, Sydney? Now, stay right here while I do something with Chad. Looks like we're all going to need a bath. Trina, go find the dog leash."

"But, Daddy, Happy doesn't like to be tied up."

Quinn glared. "Does Happy want to stay healthy? Go! Lindi, you and Syd hold on to Happy. Chad come with me, and we'll see if we can find a hose. I don't think those mud clumps will go down any drain."

"A hose! Oh boy!"

Quinn gave Sydney a helpless shrug; she returned it with a look to kill as she clutched the squirming dog.

"Sydney," Lindi offered, giggling, "you look like you have mud freckles!"

Sydney tried to smile and felt the mud tightening on her face as it dried. The smile never materialized.

Quinn returned almost immediately with the grim information. "We can't hook up because of a sewer problem."

"I thought you said we were self-contained," Sydney murmured.

"Well, heck, I didn't bring that much water in the tanks. Anyway, the bathhouse isn't far down the road. There's a hose in front of it. I'll take Chad and bring Happy along. And we need to get some fresh clothes."

"How far down the road?" Sydney stood stiffly.

"Not far." Quinn took the leash from Trina and hooked it to Happy's collar. "Yep, they have everything right there."

"Spa? Weight room? Racquetball courts? Pool? Sauna?"

"Sydney, you know they don't."

"How far, Quinn?"

"Quarter of a mile."

"Half a mile every time any one of us wants to—" Her face tightened even more, and it had nothing to do with the mud splattered all over her.

From that moment, things went downhill. After bathing five people and a dog, they found that the fishing boats were all rented. So they went hiking instead. With three exuberant children, a frisky dog, and two spirited adults, it was a miracle that they spotted a deer in the woods.

"Look, Chad!" Sydney whispered excitedly, pointing through the pines. Maybe this trip was going to be worthwhile, after all. How often did any of them get a chance to see animals in the wild?

"I wanna get real close to him!" Chad shoved the dog's leash into Sydney's hands and started running toward the wild creature.

Happy took off after Chad, jerking a surprised Sydney along with him. She tried to hang on, but the leash flew out of her hand as she was thrown against a pine tree.

"Oof!" Sydney clutched her leg and examined her stinging knee.

"Syd! You okay, honey?" Quinn knelt beside her and cradled her leg with caring hands. "Oh, it's just a little scratch. Not much damage here."

Sydney glared at the trickle of blood oozing from her knee. Yes, it was a little scratch. Nothing to be concerned about. She could have stumbled against a table in her own living room at home and done the same thing. But it didn't happen in her living room. It was a product of the camping trip, which was rapidly approaching the same status as the outdoor experience she'd endured when she was ten.

"Mom, does it hurt?" Chad's anxious little face peered into hers. "We'll put a Band-Aid on it, and that'll make it all better. Be brave."

"Be brave, Sydney," Quinn echoed with a smile and helped her to her feet.

She gave him a weary glare.

"Where's Happy?" Lindi asked.

The dog was nowhere in sight.

"I'll bet he chased the deer," Trina announced with a groan.

It took all five of them an hour to find Happy and another hour to pick all the burrs from his long golden fur.

And red Georgia clay being what it is, by the time they were ready for bed, they all needed another shower.

For Quinn and Sydney, there was no privacy. Trina and Lindi bunked together, giggling far into the night. Chad and Happy snuggled on the foldout sofa. The only beds left were narrow twin beds in the back.

Sydney tossed and turned all night. She heard every cricket and hoot owl and whippoorwill within a mile radius. When the lake frogs started their throaty chorus, she sat up in bed and hissed something obscene across the narrow isle at Quinn. Maddeningly, she could hear his steady, rhythmic breathing. He didn't even wake when the bass bullfrog joined his water-lily cronies.

She threw herself back down on the bed, flipped over, and tried again to fall asleep. In the stillness, her scratched knee began to throb. And soon she became keenly aware that her allergies were wreaking havoc on her breathing process.

Finally at four in the morning, Sydney rolled out of bed and fumbled around the kitchen looking for coffee. But with no hookups, there was no water. She settled for a glass of milk. As the soft pink threads of morning spread across the horizon, Quinn stumbled in.

"Syd, honey, you all right?" Instantly, Happy rose to greet his master.

"I just couldn't sleep."

"Any reason?"

She lifted bleary eyes. "About twenty-five. Would you like the complete list?"

"Only if I can do something about them."

"You could take us home."

"Home? You serious? We haven't even taken the kids fishing yet. It'll be better today, Syd. You'll see. I've rented two boats. And they say the perch are biting. The kids'll love it. You will, too." He pulled her into his arms and nuzzled her neck. "You're a good sport, Sydney."

Happy nuzzled her thigh. Even at five A.M. they weren't alone.

Quinn was wrong on both counts. Sydney was not a good sport and the camping trip did not get better. At noon, they were sitting in separate boats in the middle of beautiful Lake Seminole with nary a fish. Not that catching one would have made Sydney's day. She had no desire to deal with, or cook, a smelly fish. Perspiration rolled down every crevice of her body, and she knew she'd walk a mile for a cool shower—literally! Finally, Quinn motioned that it was time to come in, and she couldn't start the motor fast enough.

When she and Trina pulled their boat up to the dock, Quinn and the two little ones were already climbing out of their boat. Sydney stood up in her boat to toss the rope onto the pier, and the next thing she knew, she was choking on the less-than-clear waters of Lake Seminole.

She thrashed around and finally bobbed to the surface. Her fury was fueled by the joyful entertainment everyone else seemed to be taking from her misery.

"If you'll just stand up, Syd, you can walk out. It's real shallow here."

She glared at Quinn and let her feet settle to the murky mud bottom. As she attempted to walk out, Sydney discovered that nothing had as much suction as the red Georgia clay at the bottom of a lake. Each step was a major effort.

They all gathered around her dripping-wet form when she emerged.

"Quick way to cool off," Quinn teased.

Sydney was not amused.

"Hey, Mom, where's your other shoe?"

"Sucked into the bottom of the lake," she seethed. "A memento from me."

"Want me to try to find it?" Quinn offered.

"Never mind. I'm sure it's ruined with red clay stain, and I want nothing around to remind me of this weekend. Nothing, do you understand?" She stared heatedly at Quinn. "Right now, I'm going to walk to the showers and try to remove some of this sticky stuff. And within the hour, I expect to be speeding down the highway toward home!"

"Oh, Syd, calm down. You'll feel better when you get showered. And dried off."

"I will only feel better when I get home so I can get really clean and sleep in my own bed!"

"Syd, wait." Quinn grabbed at her hand, but she jerked it away.

"Did I ever tell you that I happen to like creature comforts, Quinn? I've had it with you and your constant playing. We just have such different habits and

127

ideas of work and play that I don't see any median ground!"

His eyes reflected the frustration he felt. "I think we both need to step back and think about this before either of us says anything else."

Sydney swallowed hard. "Maybe you're right, Quinn."

He watched her limp off wearing one tennis shoe, her dripping-wet pink-tinged T-shirt and shorts molding to her slender shoulders and hips. The Band-Aid on her knee clung by one edge and flopped with each step. Admittedly, she had taken quite a beating on this trip. Maybe it was too much to expect her to like it. Maybe he was pushing her too far too soon. Adjusting to kids, a dog, life in the great outdoors, and him wouldn't be easy for anyone. But for Syd, maybe it was impossible.

Oh God, what was he thinking? He didn't even want to think that their relationship was impossible. Maybe they did need to step back and think about it.

CHAPTER EIGHT

Sydney tried to concentrate on her new job assignment the next week. But her thoughts kept returning to Quinn. She could still see his hurt expression when she had said there was no hope for them. And his stoic, square-jawed face when he had dropped her and Chad off at their apartment with their pile of muddy camping clothes.

More than once Sydney concluded that she'd been a fool to take her frustrations out on Quinn. After all, he couldn't stop the kids and the dog from playing. He couldn't make the fish bite or hush the night noises. But a stubborn inner voice countered that the camping trip only pointed out their growing list of differences. She told Lora, but her friend adamantly opposed her reasoning.

"I'm telling you, you're making a giant mistake, Sydney."

"The mistake was going camping in the first place."

"No. The mistake was in not telling Quinn you're a suburbanite who's never lingered longer in the great outdoors than it takes to eat a picnic lunch."

"Lora, obviously you don't understand. The kids and dog seemed to be everywhere. Always getting into trouble and always dirty! And whenever they got into the red clay, somehow we got covered in it, too! I took four showers in two days and still came home a mess! Plus, I had to walk a half a mile each time! All that is not my idea of fun, while Quinn seemed to enjoy every moment."

"The price you paid for cleanliness was astounding." Lora clucked her tongue. "But is that any reason to dump the best-looking, richest hunk this side of the Suwannee River?"

"Quinn just took it all in stride." Sydney propped her fists on her hips. "If you could have seen him laughing at me when I fell into that lake, you'd understand why I'm still angry. It ruined my clothes. Stained them pink, and I couldn't get it out. He actually thought it was funny."

"Sounds like a little ego problem to me, Sydney."

"Just how do you figure that? What does ego have to do with a camping weekend?"

"Well, this is an area he enjoys and knows well. Perhaps if you'd been honest with Quinn and told him you had no skills or interest in being rough and ready, you could have been spared the misery."

"I didn't want to disappoint Chad." *Or Quinn,* she almost added.

"Oh, you didn't disappoint him. He had a ball. In fact, I'll bet all the kids did. Even the dog. But, Syd, was it worth losing Quinn to give Chad a good time?"

"It showed me that our interests are too dissimilar for any kind of compatibility, Lora. Anyway, what difference would it have made if I had told him? I still would have made the trip. And had a terrible experience."

"I'm sure things would have been different if you'd confessed your true feelings to Quinn. But it isn't too late. I'll bet you haven't talked to him all week."

Sydney shook her head glumly. "He hasn't called. Just sent me a pair of tennis shoes."

"You lost me there. Tennis shoes?"

"I left one in the lake. The mud created such a suction, it pulled my shoe off when I tried to walk. It was unbelievably awful."

"So he sent you another pair?" Lora couldn't control a spontaneous giggle. "Now that's what I call a man with a sense of humor."

"They're gorgeous shoes. Much better than the one I left in the bottom of Lake Seminole. They were all gift-wrapped and had a note that said, 'I owe you one. But here's two that match.'" Sydney grinned involuntarily, then straightened quickly. "But a sense of humor wears thin at four in the morning when you haven't slept a wink and an obnoxiously sweet dog nudges your knee to take him for a walk and you've washed him and three kids twice in the last eight hours."

"It would seem to me that that's when you'd need a sense of humor most." Lora leaned on the counter. "Why don't you call him, Sydney?"

"What would I say? 'Thanks for a perfectly miserable weekend to celebrate my graduation. I'll never forget it! Matches my black eye.'"

"Sydney, I'm sure his weekend was equally miserable. He was just a better sport about it."

Sydney stomped around the room. "Hey, Lora, you're *my* friend. I thought you were on my side."

"I am, Syd. And I see how miserable you've been

over this whole mess with Quinn this week." She paused to water a potted plant sitting on the end of the counter. "Why don't you just go out to his house and talk to him?"

Sydney ran her hands through her thick mass of auburn hair. "Lora, for someone who's so cynical about men, you certainly are being pushy."

"Don't forget, Quinn Robinson meets my criteria," Lora claimed with a wicked smile. "He's rich. He's also sexy."

"Lora!" Sydney shook her head in dismay.

"I forgot handsome, in a rugged sort of way."

"What about a strong relationship? What about love?"

Lora folded her arms across her chest. Now they were getting somewhere. "Do you love Quinn Robinson, Sydney?"

"I—I don't know, Lora. He makes me feel like no other man ever has, including Daniel."

"Well, that does it," Lora claimed. "Feeling is better than not feeling, I always say. Maybe love has something to do with all your misery, Sydney."

"He is kinda cute in shorts and a T-shirt teaching the kids to fish," Sydney admitted with a smile. "But that doesn't mean I love him."

"I think you'd better get out there and talk to that man now, Syd."

"Maybe you're right." Sydney sighed heavily. "If I bring a pizza over, can Chad eat supper with you? I won't be gone long."

"Of course. If you decide to stay the night, just call."

* * *

Sydney felt a little nervous as she drove the thirty minutes from town to Quinn's lake house. She wasn't sure what she'd say to him or how he'd react. But Lora was right. They needed to talk.

An unfamiliar Buick station wagon was parked in the driveway. When Sydney rang the doorbell, a very attractive blonde opened the door. A hundred thoughts flew through Sydney's head, and none of them were decent.

"I—uh, I'm looking for Quinn."

"He isn't here." The woman smiled patronizingly. Although quite pretty, she definitely had a supercilious air about her. "Can I help you?"

"No. I need to see him. When will he be back?"

"I'm not sure, actually. He was gone when I arrived."

"I see." Immediately, Sydney knew she did not like this woman. Yet there was something vaguely familiar about her.

"Did he know you were coming?"

"No. I just thought I'd catch him."

The woman crooked her head slightly and let her eyes slide over Sydney. "With Quinn, it doesn't really matter, does it? He just extends a standing invitation."

"Oh?" Sydney stiffened but tried to control her body language. "Well, I wasn't aware of that."

The woman laughed easily. "You must be one of Quinn's new, uh, friends."

Sydney's green eyes narrowed. "And you must be one of his, uh, old ones?" She felt justified in questioning this strange woman in Quinn's house. After all,

133

enduring a camping weekend must qualify her for something. Maybe the boob of the year award.

The woman faked laughter. "You have a way with words. Don't worry about my being here. I don't really count. I'm Stacey Robinson, Quinn's ex. I'm sure he's told you about our strange, amiable relationship." She pursed her lips into a pout. "Whenever I'm in town, I always stay here. One thing about Quinn is that he's wonderfully generous. Shares anything he has."

"Yes, I noticed that." Sydney could feel herself growing hot under the collar. "How convenient that he just leaves the place open for you."

"Well, not exactly open. I have a key."

"Handy."

"Yes, it is. I know I'll always have a place here."

"I'm glad I had this chance to talk to you, Stacey." Sydney took a backward step.

"Who shall I tell Quinn came by?"

"Oh, don't bother. I'll reach him another time." Sydney paused, then reached down and jerked off her fancy tennis shoes. Shoving them into the surprised Stacey's hands, she said, "Tell him he knows what he can do with these shoes. He'll know who sent them."

She marched away in sock feet, practically dove into her car, and pressed the accelerator, praying she wouldn't pass a cop on the way home.

Nineteen minutes later, Sydney burst into Lora's apartment without knocking.

Lora, who sat cross-legged on the floor in front of the TV with Chad, looked up in surprise. "Back so soon?"

"You bet! Boy! Am I glad I went out there!"

134

"I knew you would be." Lora's voice was warm and confident.

"Hi, Mom," Chad greeted her casually. "We're watching TV. Come on and have some pizza with us."

"No thank you, Chad. I have some nails to chew on." She whirled around and headed across the hall to her own apartment.

Lora caught up with her at the door. "Did I hear you right?"

"Yeah! Got any nails you want chewed?"

"Not at the moment. What happened, Sydney?"

"That louse! Who the hell does he think he is? Following me around town, dragging me through the mud with the kids and dog, just pretending to be one big happy family! He's nothing but a lying, cheating, dirty-dealing gigolo!"

Lora's hand shot out to clamp against Sydney's lips. "I can see you're a little upset. But your young son is in the next room, and I don't want him to hear such language, even if his mother doesn't care."

"Oh, Lora, I don't know when I've been so mad!" Sydney's eyes filled with tears, and she fought futilely against them. "I—oh!"

"Come on in the kitchen and let me get you something. We can talk in there." Lora put an arm around her friend's shoulder and steered her back into the apartment.

Sydney stared at the steaming mug of coffee for a long time before she said a word. "I can't believe it."

Lora fixed herself a cup and slid onto the stool next to Sydney. "Okay, shoot. But keep your voice down."

"I'd like to shoot Quinn Robinson right in the caboose!"

"Good beginning, Syd. Now would you please tell me what this is all about? Did you see Quinn?"

"No. I saw the one who keeps his home fires burning."

"What? Who is she?"

"Oh, they're just one little happy family, all right."

"Who, Sydney?"

"There she was, blond, with an hourglass figure, waiting for Quinn to return from the ravages of some strenuous game off in the hinterlands. No doubt some tournament where he struggled all day to hit that poor little ball into a cup! Life's hell, ain't it?"

Lora scratched her forehead. "You left me somewhere between the golf course and the hinterlands."

"She's at his house right now, waiting for him."

"Who is?"

The words almost exploded from Sydney. "His ex, that's who! She informed me she had a bed there just any ol' time she desires—and apparently she isn't the only one. Quinn is *so generous,* don't you think? Now isn't that handy?"

"Um, yes. You sure?"

"I talked to her. She just popped in and doesn't know where he is because he wasn't there when she arrived. But that doesn't matter. They have a special arrangement. She has a key."

"Tell you what, Sydney. I think this calls for wine, not coffee." Lora whisked the cups away and set a half-empty bottle of Chablis on the counter between them.

"I'd like to bean him with that bottle," Sydney grumbled.

"No, no, wait until we empty it!" Lora cautioned

with a grim smile. "Then I'll help you! Damn that creep, anyway!"

Sydney turned and wagged her finger. "Now it's your turn to watch your language, Lora. My son's in the next room!"

Their eyes met and the two old friends laughed and Lora poured their wineglasses full. "We'll do this quietly. Here's to finding out about a first-class jerk before it was too late."

"Amen." Sydney took a big gulp and tried to pretend it didn't matter that Quinn had a live-in relationship with his former wife.

It was Friday night before Quinn called. "I've been out of town. Found your tennis shoes in the laundry room. What's wrong? Didn't they fit?"

"Did you also get my message telling you exactly what you can do with them?"

"Sydney? Is that you? My sweet—"

"Damn right it is! Takes me awhile, but I do catch on. I met your ex-wife."

"Stacey? Where?"

"As if you didn't know! Convenient relationship you have with her, Quinn. I wish you'd told me before I went to bed with you! That's just not my style!" She slammed the phone down and fought the tears welling behind her angry eyes.

CHAPTER NINE

"I don't sleep with her, Sydney!"

"Did I ask?"

Quinn loomed large and powerful in Sydney's room, making her small apartment seem even smaller. He exuded energy and anger. The expanse of his shoulders stretched his knit shirt taut enough to outline the curves of his chest muscles. Curly chest hair edged his shirt's neck opening, and Sydney longed to bury her face against that strong chest. With difficulty, she maintained an indifferent facade.

"You didn't have to ask."

Her eyes snapped back to his square-jawed face, and she drew herself up defiantly. "How interesting that you're capable of mind reading. Did you also decipher that I don't go for man sharing?"

"Sydney, I want to explain my relationship with Stacey."

"Her presence in your home explained all I need to know. She called your relationship strange and amiable."

"Well, I suppose it is. She stays in my house when she's in town. Her father's ill, in a nursing home here.

138

And she comes frequently to see him. It doesn't make sense for her to stay in a motel."

"So you give her the key to your house?"

He spread his large hands before her. "Why not? The house is big, lots of rooms. Hell, I'm gone half the time." His blue eyes implored her to understand.

Sydney forced a smile. "How altruistic of you. She said you were a generous man. Generous with everything!"

His hands gripped her arms fiercely. "She's the mother of my children, for God's sake! But not my lover. You are, Sydney." He pulled her roughly against him and clamped his lips on hers, hard and demanding. The kiss was hot and desperate, embodying conflicting passions of frustration and desire as he drew her closer with undeniable urgency.

Sydney didn't pull back. She couldn't. She melted against Quinn, wanting to believe his claims. His kiss blocked out all else for the moment, even the doubts. She accepted the strength of his kiss, marveling at the heightened sensations she felt whenever he was near. Vitality. Energy. Anticipation of something wonderful, something exciting.

In her weakened state, Sydney responded to the message she received from his body and kiss. In his actions, she perceived desperation, a yearning beyond his control. He had driven over immediately and had filled the room with his anger, ranting and raving like a raging bull. Then he couldn't stay away from her, couldn't contain his hunger for her kiss. But did he do this with Stacey—and others?

Sydney stifled the grievous thought. His lips were firmly intended just for her.

139

As he held her in his arms, she agonized at the idea of Quinn's hands on anyone else. She wanted to think she was the only woman in his life. She wanted to be the one and only woman for him! She loved him so!

His hands spread over her back, molding her to his entire hard length. Quinn wanted to possess her, to capture her forever, to force her into his arms. He hated the doubt and mistrust in her misty green eyes yet took encouragement from her anger. It wouldn't have mattered who he bedded if she didn't care at all. But she did. He determined to show her his feelings, how much he cared.

Like someone drowning, Sydney clung to his strength, wrapping her arms around his shoulders, feeling the tautness at his neck. Her fingers dug into his dark curls. Indeed, she was sinking in the deluge of Quinn's overwhelming presence.

She was weak when it came to Quinn Robinson, but dear God, she wanted him with a need she'd never before experienced. Wanted him all to herself, wanted him to hold her, to soothe her doubts, to give her strength. To make love to her.

"Oh, Syd," he breathed. "I don't ever want you to doubt it. You're the only woman for me."

"Don't, Quinn." She pushed against him, struggling to make herself resist him. "Please don't kiss me like that."

"I can't help it, Syd. I want you."

She drew in a quick breath. "Is that the way you are with all your women? Can't help it?"

His blue eyes hardened, and he shoved her away. "I told you, there are no others! You have to believe me, Sydney."

140

Her brain whirled with the range of emotions she'd experienced in the last few moments. Jealousy at the notion of Stacey in Quinn's bed. Anger when she thought he made love to another woman. Desire when she was drawn into his arms. Fear that she was losing him. Yet encompassing it all was an inner voice warning her to protect herself from further pain.

"I'm trying to believe you, Quinn."

"Stacey and I have an unusual relationship, I'll admit. It's probably better now than it ever was when we were married. You saw what she's like. Surely you can understand what I mean. I just—we couldn't get along on a full-time basis." He walked around the room, filling it with his excess energy as he talked. "I traveled too much. She was at home with the babies. We grew apart. She has a different philosophy from mine. But she's a good mother to the girls. And now, with her father ill here in Tallahassee, I figured the least I could do was to give her a place to stay."

Sydney approached him. "Quinn. It's all right. I understand, I think."

"I want you to know where I stand, Sydney."

"You don't have to explain. I have no ties on you. No commitment, right, Quinn?" Her green eyes met his steadily.

"Do you want a commitment?"

"I don't believe in it." She spoke stubbornly, defensively. "It doesn't work."

"I wish I could convince you differently."

"You?" She laughed softly. "The man who wanted sex with no strings attached? The man who generously shares his home with a former wife and God knows

141

who else? You're going to teach me about commitment?"

"Sydney Jacques, you infuriate me! But right now, I only know I want you so much, it's hard for me to stand here two feet away from you."

She pursed her lips. "Your self-control is commendable."

"Where's Chad?"

"With his dad."

Quinn's eyes flickered. "For the night?"

She nodded.

"The last time that happened, you called up in a panic. Don't you need to talk about it this time?"

She took a deep breath. "You were right. It gets easier. I didn't even go crazy about the blazing redhead Daniel brought along this time."

"Then we're alone?"

"For the whole weekend." She swallowed and reached out to take his hand. "Quinn, I want—I want you, too."

With a low groan from deep in his chest, he hauled her into the fortress of his arms and pressed her against him. "Syd, my sweet Syd . . . I need you."

He buried his face in the thick tangle of her hair. The soft curls reminded him of the delicate fragrance of orchids. And she was just as delicate. Her fragility was well-hidden behind her tough exterior, but he knew what was beneath. A dewy-eyed woman who lived her commitments, even though she denied it. A woman desired a commitment from her man, even though she disclaimed it.

His lips kissed a moist trail along her neck, then up to her chin, then to her parted lips. She was waiting and eager for him. And he devoured her, encasing her in his strong arms, making sure she knew the strength of his desire.

He pulled back and looked at her with a touch of wildness in his blue eyes. He wanted her, oh how he wanted her! Like none other! Maybe she was different .from all the others. While Sydney could be sassy and always a challenge, she could also be wonderful and warm. He needed her terribly.

She stood before him, willing and eager, her arms lifted to accept him, inviting. Quivering slightly in her thin, flowered blouse and those sexy white shorts that hugged her behind, her body seemed to beckon him, enticing, seductive, pleading.

Her hands fluttered to her breasts and began unbuttoning her blouse. Inch by alluring inch, the flowered material parted to reveal her creamy skin, the defined hollow, the pale twins burgeoning within easy reach. Their gentle rise and fall was mesmerizing, their rosebud tips blossoming rich and delectable, ripe for the plucking.

Impatiently, Quinn pushed the flowers away and centered his palms over those thriving buds, opening his tanned fingers to encompass both satiny globes. He dug into their softness. They were plump and warm and the nipples were hot and hard, revealing the passion simmering inside her. He rubbed over them, back and forth, building friction to the point of combustion.

Sydney shrugged the blouse off her shoulders, and the flowers dropped like discarded petals to the floor. All Quinn could think of was the expanse of softly feminine flesh before him, and he began a sensuous caressing, trailing his hands over every inch of her arms and shoulders, breasts, and ribs. His hands reached around to her back, and he pressed sweet, moist kisses to her breasts. As he nibbled her gently, tasting the freshness of her skin, he was accosted by the exquisitely faint fragrance of orchids.

She arched her breasts, and her head rolled back in a gesture of ecstasy. The sweet globes thrust forward, and he ravished one, then the other, as if he couldn't get enough of her. His tongue licked a moist trail over each swollen mound, pausing to taste each rose-tipped nipple before dipping to the heated hollow between them.

Quinn breathed heavily against skin as he planted hot kisses to her pounding heart. His hands stroked her back, then came around to the front of her shorts. His fingers found her zipper and slowly slid it down. Then his hand pushed the shorts and panties from her slender hips.

The flimsy items dropped swiftly down those long legs, and she stepped out of them. His fingers gently caressed her inner thighs, and she moaned softly. Then she pushed his hand away. "Now it's my turn."

Her hands slid beneath his knit skirt and around his waist, then up to the ribs. Her fingernails raked across his skin, relishing the muscular maleness of him, the firm belly, the smattering of hair. Eager fingers followed the hairy trail up his middle, shoving the shirt past his ribs to the rounded muscles of his chest. She paused to rub across the tiny pearled nipples. Again she fondled them, then spontaneously bent her head and kissed them, licking and tasting his skin.

With a quick intake of air, Quinn tore off his shirt,

and it joined her flowered blouse on the floor, forgotten.

She continued kissing his chest, taking each beaded nipple between her teeth, biting gently on them. Her lips throbbed with the pounding of his heart and moved to the rhythm of his heavy breathing. His musky fragrance was heady and intoxicating.

Suddenly he moved back and stepped out of his jeans. When he returned within her reach, he stood nude, his desire for her obvious. Sydney's green eyes grew dark as she admired his masculine body, resplendent in all its glory.

"Oh, Quinn," she murmured as her hands strayed over him.

"Syd, Syd—" He spoke her name raggedly and rested his large hands on her shoulders, urging her to touch him.

She knelt before him, caressing and kissing him until he was nearly crazy with desire. He reached down and lifted her in his arms.

"Yes, yes," she whispered against his neck as he made his way down the hall to her bedroom.

He eased them down onto the bed and smothered her with kisses. "Syd, I can't wait for you."

Assertively, she pushed him back and covered him with her body. "You're all mine tonight, Quinn!"

"Syd, oh Syd, love me! Don't stop."

She framed his pale hips with her knees and gripped his shoulders. "I do . . . love you . . . Quinn." Her voice gave way to a soft moan as their heated flesh met —and merged.

She was wild and uninhibited.

He was passionate and uncontrolled.

They rode to passion's summit rapidly and in unison, then clutched each other fiercely.

"Syd, my love—"

"Quinn, oh, oh—"

She slumped onto his chest, and heat radiated through her. She felt the steady pounding of his heart. His arms embraced her, and he rolled her down so they were side by side on the bed. They lay together for a long time, enjoying the lazy pleasure of the warm afterglow.

They made love again, this time leisurely, luxuriously. Sydney gloried in the magnificence of his body, admiring and stroking the taut masculine planes. She'd never been so free and uninhibited.

Quinn worked with slow deliberation to arouse her, teasing and exploring her body until she begged for him. He made it perfectly clear that he was there for her pleasure. Her joy was his. Did she like this? Or this?

Finally, in a frenzy, they rose again to ecstasy.

Afterward, they lay breathlessly in each other's arms.

"Come home with me tonight, Syd. Spend the weekend at my house. I want you to feel comfortable there, to be familiar with the whole place." His hand stroked her bare back. "I'd like to make love to you in every room."

She laughed. "Well, I'd surely know them intimately then."

His voice rumbled through her. "I want you in every room in the house. In the Florida room overlooking the lake. In my bedroom overlooking the pool. On the balcony overlooking the living room—"

"I'm exhausted before we get there!"

"I think you can keep up with me," he murmured.

"What about—what about *her* room?"

"Whose?" He shifted and looked into her eyes with dark conviction. "Her room first."

"Promise?"

"I swear, Syd." His lips propelled against hers in a driving kiss.

They showered together and rescued their clothes from her living-room floor. On the way out of town, they stopped long enough to pick up a Chinese takeout supper. It was dark when they arrived, but Quinn showed her how the lovely views from every window were visible with floodlights. In the Florida room, they sat on floor pillows and fed each other egg rolls and moo shu pork with plum sauce.

Then he took her hand and led her down the hall to the immaculate and seldom-used room located in the back of the house.

"Here first."

"Are you sure?"

"I'm positive." He peeled off his shirt. "How else can I convince you I don't give a damn about her? Or any other woman! Just you, Syd." With one vicious motion, he yanked the pristine bedspread off the bed and threw it into the corner. Then he turned to her. "It's only you, Syd."

Her green eyes darkened as he reached for her.

The next day, they walked every inch of Quinn's lakeside property. Huge water oaks dripping with Spanish moss meandered all the way to the lake's edge, and pink and white azaleas checkered every path. Quinn beat her soundly in a game of tennis and took her rowing on the lake as retribution. Then they cooled off in the sparkling pool.

"I think that's the first time I've seen you in a boat when you haven't gone overboard," Quinn teased as he brought out a float for each of them.

"Maybe I'm learning," she giggled and heaved herself onto the floating mattress.

"I had the fishnet ready."

"Thanks for the vote of confidence."

"I'd like to get the girls a small catamaran when they're a little older. Then they can go sailing on the lake."

"Your children are very lucky to have you for a father, Quinn."

"I want to make sure they have a fun childhood in spite of the divorce."

Sydney smiled warmly. "Well, I'm sure they do. They have everything they could possibly want, Quinn. Including love."

His blue eyes grew thoughtful. "That's the most important of all, you know. The love."

"What was your childhood like, Quinn?"

He chuckled dryly. "It was nothing like theirs. No fun at all. Not much love, either. Rough." He paused reflectively. "I had an unpleasant childhood."

"Did you grow up here in Florida?"

"No. My family lived in Detroit. My mother died when I was five or six. I struggled along with my dad, picking up odd jobs on the streets until I was about twelve. Then I—" He halted.

"Go on. You were twelve, and—?"

"I ran away. My father became abusive. And drunk

148

most of the time. So I left. During the next few years, my life wasn't much better. A variety of foster homes. Finally, a friend and I plotted our getaway and left for Florida."

"Why Florida?"

"You know how kids dream about someplace better? Florida was our dream place. We took a bus south and went as far as our money would take us. That was Jacksonville. We heard about jobs available in Tallahassee, so we hitchhiked over here."

"Did you get jobs?"

"Sure did. Caddying at every golf course in town."

"Is that where your interest in golfing started?"

"Yep. I learned by watching for months before I ever touched a club, other than to hand it to someone else. When I saw that some people got paid for playing or teaching people to play golf, I realized it might be my way out. So I went back to high school and ended up getting a golfing scholarship to the university."

"That must have been very difficult for you to do." Sydney's eyes softened as she looked at Quinn with a new light. "It was a struggle, wasn't it, Quinn? Not just making it big, but surviving."

His float turned around in slow circles. "While you were going to summer camp and playing dolls, I was selling newspapers on the corner in Detroit."

Sydney slid off her mattress and, with her body in the water, circled his waist with her arms. "You actually had no childhood, did you, Quinn?"

His smile was tight. "Not much. But I've been making up for lost time. I suppose that's why I have all these toys."

Her green eyes misted at the thought of a young

149

Quinn, cold and unhappy. "That's why you have to share everything."

He leaned down to her. "Everything but you, Syd. I don't think I could bear the thought of sharing you."

"You don't have to, Quinn."

He drew closer, and as his lips met hers, he slid off the mattress. Melded together in the kiss, they sank into the sparkling waters of the pool and emerged moments later, laughing and clinging to one another.

Laughing and clinging the whole weekend.

CHAPTER TEN

When Sydney opened her eyes Sunday morning, she found herself wrapped in Quinn's strong arms and pressed against the sturdy wall of his chest. A warm, musky fragrance surrounded them, creating an aura of security and comfort. She inhaled deeply, as if trying to absorb all the wonderful aspects about Quinn that she loved. She let her breath out in tiny spurts, trying not to exhale all the joy he gave her.

She watched his bare chest rise and fall with each regular breath and wondered about his love. He'd never actually said it. She wondered, too, about her own feelings. Was she just overwhelmed by a man who was so different from any she had ever known that her desire was confused with love? And always in her heart was the question, Was she setting herself up for more hurt?

She slid gently out of his arms and watched with envy as he nuzzled the pillow. His lips were slightly parted, as if ready to taste her again. It was all she could do to keep from waking him with her kisses and sliding back into the fortress of his arms. And loving him again.

But she needed some time alone. Time to think. Af-

151

ter climbing from their warm bed, Sydney found a thick, terry-cloth shirt in the bathroom and slid her arms into the roomy sleeves. It hit her midthigh, and she felt good just knowing that Quinn wore it, too. Padding barefoot through the big empty house, she admitted that the entire weekend with Quinn had been so wonderful, she didn't even care that it was raining. Now was a good time to think.

She watched the drops making pockmarks in puddles in the yard and remembered that she usually hated rain. It reminded her too much of the day Daniel had left her. But today she didn't mind the rain. Suddenly she was struck with the realization that she didn't even care that Daniel was gone from her life. At one time, she'd thought she couldn't live without him. It was strange to acknowledge that she was making it very well without him, that she had other things to fill the heartbreaking gap he'd left.

Most of all, she had her self-respect. She was proud of her recent accomplishments, the graduation and new job. Chad was her heart's delight. And Quinn? Quinn was . . . her love.

On this rainy Sunday morning, she knew she loved him.

Smiling to herself, Sydney wandered into the kitchen and put on the coffee. While it brewed, she opened the double-doored pantry. Amazingly, it was well stocked. As her eyes traveled over cans and cake mixes, she remembered Quinn saying that he wanted always to have plenty of food for the girls or for guests whenever they might pop in. Plenty of food for everyone. It occurred to her that, as a child, he probably had never had enough food. And never had a pantry that looked like this one.

She pictured a scruffy kid with piercing blue eyes and curly dark hair, needing a haircut. Standing on a cold, windy street corner in the city . . . selling newspapers . . . a torn, too-small jacket . . . constantly hungry. Sydney shook her head to dispel the image. With all the wealth around her, it was hard to believe that Quinn grew up so tough. And yet she knew that that was why he surrounded himself with plenty of food and love.

She had never suffered for those things as a child. There had always been plenty of both food and love for her and her sister. They even had a wonderful Sunday morning tradition of baking something special. Spontaneously, Sydney reached for a cake mix and selected cans of crushed pineapple and cherries. Humming, she dug around until she found a small package of chopped pecans, and she began to mix a Sunday-morning special for Quinn.

When Quinn awakened and staggered into the kitchen, a marvelous aroma greeted him. Sydney sat hunched on one of the Florida-room sofas, cuddling a cup of coffee, watching the rain. He approached from the back and kissed her neck. "Morning, honey."

She leaned back and returned the kiss, upside down. He was bare-chested and wore only shorts.

Laughing, he caressed her face. "The smells coming from the kitchen are enough to wake a grizzly! What have you been up to this morning?"

"Watching the rain. And fixing you a Sunday-morning special."

"What's that?" He chuckled and headed for the coffee.

Sydney joined him and began to dish up the steaming, savory cake. "When I was a kid, my mother always baked something delectable on Sunday mornings. As my sis and I grew up, it became a tradition that we shared. Sometimes we tried a new recipe, but our all-time favorite was what we called a Dump Cake. So I made you one."

He leaned back onto the counter and watched her, smiling. "A Sunday-morning special, huh? Sounds like a great tradition for a family to have. It sure smells like heaven."

"It's so easy, Trina and Lindi could make it. A can of cherry pie filling, a drained can of crushed pineapple, chopped pecans, and yellow cake mix. Usually I add shredded coconut, but I couldn't find any in your pantry."

He stopped her and framed her face with his large hands. "You're beautiful, you know that?"

"Because I can throw together a mean cake?" She tried to laugh off his compliment.

"No. Because of this." His lips glazed over hers, then kissed her cheeks, eyes, and nose. "Because of the way I feel when I'm with you. Because of the special things you do. The way you are."

"It's been a wonderful weekend, Quinn."

"No regrets about coming out here?" His thumbs caressed her cheeks.

"Only that it has to end."

"It doesn't have to, you know. Stay on, Syd."

She twisted out of his arms. "I have to get home

154

soon, Quinn. Daniel will be bringing Chad back around noon, and—"

"That isn't what I meant, Syd."

Nervously she picked up the two plates heaped with cake. "I have lots to do this afternoon to get ready for work. Laundry and groceries for the week. And I haven't touched the apartment in days. It's a mess."

He refilled both their coffee cups and followed her silently into the Florida room. "I don't have a thing to do this week. Wouldn't it be nice if we—"

She held her hand up, interrupting. "Quinn, I can't. I have work. I don't have time to play. I know that's something you can't understand, but I actually like my job. In fact, I'm liking it better than I ever dreamed I would."

He walked to the window and stood staring out at the rain pouring onto the patio and peppering the once-sparkling pool. "I envy you that enthusiasm, Syd." His voice was pensive and hollow.

She stopped and looked at him, aghast. "You envy *me*, Quinn? I, who have nothing? Why, Quinn Robinson, you have everything anyone could want!"

His blue eyes pierced into her soul, his words into her heart. "No, Syd. I do not have everything anyone could want."

"Why, you've achieved complete success in your field, Quinn." She walked around, gesturing at the room. "Your home is practically a mansion on the enviable Lakeshore Drive. You have two beautiful daughters. Everything!"

"But everything you mentioned has already been accomplished. The present is stagnant. My future—" He shrugged. "Uncertain."

"Quinn, you deserve everything you have, including the time to sit back and enjoy life. And play." She took him in her arms, cradling his head.

"I want you, Syd. I *need* you." Even as he felt her warmth, he knew that having her wasn't really enough. The trouble he felt was deep inside his own heart. He desperately needed her, but he also needed more. And he knew the answers had to come from himself.

Sydney's only response was to pull him closer to her breast.

That night as Sydney tucked Chad into bed, she thought of the young Quinn Robinson, the kid who had had no mother to give him the measure of love kids need. She squeezed Chad tightly and gave him an extra kiss.

"Pooh! You're smothering me, Mom!" He struggled against her. "What was all that for?"

"Oh, just because I love you, Chad. And I'm glad to have you back home."

He snuggled against his pillow. "I'm glad to be back home, too."

She smiled with relief and ruffled his hair. Deep down, she knew she worried that Chad would like it better with his father than with her. The divorce had created a natural competition between her and Daniel for Chad's affection. And that was all wrong. A father and mother shouldn't have to compete for love. Maybe Quinn and his ex-wife had the best arrangement, after all.

During the next few weeks at work, Sydney became more involved with planning and producing the community affairs programs. Dixie proved to be a good teacher, and she sought Sydney's opinions for future shows. They discussed options, and it was Sydney's job to research them and report back to Dixie.

Sydney leafed through sections of her folder. "Here's a great one. A ninety-seven-year-old man who still works as a blacksmith, shoeing horses. He's an amazing man, steady and strong. And this one's about a lady who raises bean sprouts in big trays in her back bedroom. Uses her kids' old bunk bed frames to hold the trays. Did you know bean sprouts don't need sunlight? Only water. Cute story." She paused and lifted another page. "But this one's the best. It's about the Rainbow Bunch."

Dixie raised her head curiously. "Rainbow Bunch? I've heard something about them, but I can't remember what."

Sydney sat on the edge of her chair and began to explain. "They're a nonprofit organization who work on various projects for kids with cancer. Some of the members are former cancer patients. Last year they bought new toys and equipment for the hospital playground. Their new project is a large one. They need to purchase a permanent campsite for a summer camp for the kids."

"So what could we do?"

"One Sunday each month, they have a party for those kids who are in the hospital. Cake and clowns and ice cream and a special performance, like a magician or trained dog act. Sometimes kids who aren't in the hospital return for the party. It's very festive, and we could film it. Using that as a backdrop, we could have a few interviews and discuss their financial needs. But mostly we could show the kids having fun."

"Do you think it would be okay to take the cameras to the hospital, Sydney?"

"I think it would be the best way possible to acquaint the public with the great things the Rainbow Bunch is doing for a terrific group of kids."

Dixie nodded. "Okay. Go to it. We'll schedule filming on Sunday. You set it up, Sydney."

"Me?"

"Is there another Sydney in here? Of course, you! It's the best way to get your feet wet, Syd. If you need any help, I'm always available."

"Oh, Dixie, thanks!" Sydney fairly sailed out of the office and, seated at her own tiny desk, began making phone calls. The first was to Quinn.

"It'll be my first solo effort! Oh, Quinn, I'm so excited!"

"I'm very happy for you, Syd. Sounds terrific!"

"Why don't you bring Lindi and Trina over to the hospital on Sunday? They can join their little friend, Beth, in the fun. And they can see themselves on TV later."

He was quiet for a few moments. "I don't think we can make it on Sunday, Syd."

"But I thought the girls were there with you, and you didn't have a thing planned. They'll love it, Quinn. How often do they get to be on TV?"

"Tell you what. I'll talk to them and get back to you. But don't plan on us."

Before she could protest further, he hung up. She was still puzzling over Quinn's strange reaction when he called back ten minutes later.

"Sydney, you were right about the girls. When I told them about it, they were thrilled."

"Great, Quinn! I wanted you to meet the organizers of the Rainbow Bunch anyway. It's a fine organization, and they do a valuable community service. You won't regret coming."

"Yeah, well, I hope not."

Quinn refused to discuss the subject further, even when they went out to eat later in the week. On the day of the party, Sydney was running around like a crazy person, trying to make sure everything was perfect. They'd set the party up downstairs in one of the hospital's larger conference rooms because once word got around that TV cameras would be there, everyone wanted to come.

Kids were everywhere, some in wheelchairs looking very sick, others looking perfectly normal. Many wore cute and clever hats or wigs to hide their baldness, but some were just themselves. Sydney had almost decided that Quinn had changed his mind and wasn't bringing the girls, after all, when they appeared in the doorway.

"Hi! It's almost time to start. Come on, girls. Chad's over here with Beth." She paused momentarily and glanced up at Quinn. "Glad you brought them."

"You girls go on. I'll stay here." He gestured and accidentally nudged a little boy standing behind him. "Oh, sorry, son. You okay?"

"I'm fine. Just don't knock the needle out," the boy said, pointing to his wrist where an IV tube was attached.

Quinn swallowed hard and watched silently as the boy moved toward the ice cream, pushing the IV stand.

Sydney smiled grimly and steered Lindi and Trina toward the others. She had too much to do today to worry about Quinn. If he wanted to stand around and stare, she couldn't help it. The best she could do was to flash him a smile occasionally.

Quinn stood by the door, uncharacteristically not involving himself in any of the festivities.

Midway through the party, Sydney approached him with another man in tow. "Quinn, I want you to meet Scott Rogers, the president of the Rainbow Bunch. His son is one of the kids who made it. He's in college now. Scott, this is Quinn Robinson."

Scott extended his hand. "Quinn Robinson, what a pleasure. I've watched you win golf tournaments for years!"

Quinn nodded his appreciation and shook hands.

"Sydney tells me," Scott said, "that you might be interested in working with our kids. Boy, do we need all kinds of help!"

Quinn looked quickly at Sydney. She smiled encouragingly and mumbled something about having lots of work to do before slipping away and leaving the men to talk alone.

When the filming was over and the party was drawing to a close, Sydney ambled over to the door where Quinn had remained. "Well, I think it went okay. How about from your view by the door, Quinn?"

His mouth was tight. "I'm sure the film part will be just fine, Syd. You seem to know what you're doing. I just don't like to be set up."

"What?"

"And you even used my kids to get me here."

"Oh, you didn't want to come?" She waved good-

160

bye to some of the participating children and parents. "Quinn, look—"

"No, *you* look, Sydney Jacques. Just who the hell do you think you are, trying to manipulate me like this?"

"I'm not sure I know what you're talking about, Quinn. You said you weren't busy today. And the girls wanted to come."

"So you took it on yourself to give me something to do. Thanks a helluva lot, Syd. What made you think I could help these kids? What do I know about any of this?"

Her green eyes hardened. "They really need people to help, people who care. I thought you might be interested if you could see all these kids—"

"Spare me your speech, Sydney. We aren't on camera now!"

"You listen to me, dammit, Quinn! The kind of campsite they need costs lots of money. But that's not why I asked you to come today. The Rainbow Bunch is a group of people who care and realize that these kids are just like any others. They need love and—"

"Oh no, they aren't like any others, Sydney! They're sick!"

"Sick and funny-looking." Sydney drew closer and eyed him steadily. "Admit it, Quinn. When they lose their hair and gain weight from the chemotherapy, they don't look normal. But they are. You can tell yourself differently, but you're wrong. They want to have fun, attend school, and go to camp just like any other kid."

Quinn took a shaky breath. "But they're not like any other kids. They're very ill. Don't you think it breaks my heart to see them?"

161

"Then go out there in the hall and cry for them! Meanwhile, some people will be in here facing whatever must be faced. And some people will have fun with them. And some people will watch them grow up and live normal lives."

"It isn't for me."

"Quinn, they aren't all doing to die."

He turned away. "God, Sydney, you're blunt."

"Let's be blunt, Quinn. It's time we quit whispering about it. Do you know the survival statistics for certain kids with acute lymphatic leukemia?"

He shook his head silently.

"Many children *do* survive. Did you listen to Scott's interview? His son is one of those survivors. He's in college now. They're living, Quinn. And they just want a chance to have a little fun while they're kids."

"Daddy! Daddy!"

Their conversation was diverted by Lindi, with Chad and Trina close behind. "We had fun!"

"I can't wait to see me on TV!"

"I got chocolate ice cream on my shirt," Chad complained. "Hope it doesn't show on TV."

"Daddy, can Beth come out to play next weekend?"

Quinn looked down into the smiling faces of his healthy daughters. "Well honey, I—I don't know. We'll have to talk to her mother."

"We already asked her. She said okay."

"Oh."

Sydney leaned back and folded her arms. "Well, Quinn, what do you say? They just want to play."

His blue eyes cut into her as he answered his daughter with the classic put-off used by all parents. "We'll see, Lindi."

"It's okay, Daddy," Lindi said softly. "I'll keep an eye on her. Anyway, she's stopped taking that awful medicine that makes her hair fall out. And it's coming back!" She paused to giggle.

Quinn stared at her, horrified.

Trina added, "It's very soft and thin, like a baby's hair. She wore a wig today because of the TV, but it's hot and she doesn't like to wear it."

"She let me try it on," Lindi said proudly.

Sydney smiled. "I think we got a shot of Lindi trying on the wig. Tell your friends. Be sure to watch tonight at six thirty."

"You girls ready to go?" Quinn asked, obviously anxious to leave.

"Thanks for inviting us, Sydney," Trina said shyly. "I've never been on TV before."

"Yeah, thanks!" Lindi said exuberantly, grabbing Sydney for a big hug. "See you, Chad."

Sydney waved at Lindi and Trina, then turned to Quinn. "It's too bad you feel this way, Quinn. I thought it might be something you would find challenging."

"You thought wrong. It's something I just can't handle."

"I'm sure these kids' families felt the same way at the beginning, Quinn. But they couldn't turn their heads and look the other way. And thank God lots of other people don't turn their backs, either."

"Sydney, you don't understand. I won't turn my back on them. I'll send a check to help them. It just hurts too much to see—"

Sydney held up her hand to stop him. "Spare me, Quinn. It hurts *you* to look? Come on, Quinn! What

163

about them? Hey, just ignore today. Forget everything you've seen and what I've said. Walk away. There are two ways you could go here, Quinn. Send them a check to appease your conscience, then go fishing and forget about them. Or you could get involved and do something to help."

"Why the hell do you think you can tell me what to do?" He wheeled around and followed Lindi and Trina.

As the door slammed shut, Sydney stifled a low sob. "But you would be so good with them, Quinn. Can't you see that? I thought I knew you, Quinn. I thought I could help," she whispered. "But I figured you all wrong."

She didn't hear from Quinn all the next week. And she didn't call him. Somehow she just couldn't. Obviously she had strained their relationship to its limit. What right did she have to interfere in his life? None, and she regretted trying to influence him.

But she didn't regret doing the story on the Rainbow Bunch. Of that, she was very proud. The local newspapers had picked up stories on them, and Scott Rogers had called her to say contributions to the Rainbow Bunch's summer camp fund had doubled since the story aired.

Also, ratings for the community affairs series were soaring. Lee walked around the station with a silly grin, and he and Mr. Reinhardt even took Sydney and Dixie out to lunch one day. Her career was beginning to blossom.

Late Friday afternoon, she received a phone call from a competitive TV station in town.

"Ms. Jacques? This is Thomas Francis of WFLA. Congratulations on your fine series on the Rainbow Bunch. It was tough and hard-hitting, with just the right amounts of pathos and warmth."

Sydney's heart fluttered nervously. "Why, thank you, Mr. Francis."

"I'll get right to the point, Ms. Jacques. Our sportscaster is leaving next month, and we noticed you applied for a job with us last year. We're very interested in you and wonder if you could send us a recent tape for consideration?"

Sydney thought she'd float right up to the ceiling when she cradled the phone. Her first thought was to call Quinn. Then she remembered she couldn't call him. With her meddling, she had created such a rift in their relationship, they might never talk again.

CHAPTER ELEVEN

"Why don't you call him, Sydney?"

"I did, Lora. No answer. Only the machine. Have you ever tried to leave an apology on a machine?"

Lora folded her arms. "Is that what you want to do, Syd? Apologize?"

"Well, I did intrude in a very sensitive area for a man. I thought I knew Quinn well enough to do it. Obviously, I didn't."

Lora narrowed her hazel eyes. "Syd, you did exactly the right thing. The series on the Rainbow Bunch was hard-hitting and good. It opened everyone's eyes to their needs and accomplishments, but mostly to those brave, beautiful kids. Don't ever apologize to anyone for that. And inviting Quinn and his children along was just a bonus for them."

"I hoped Quinn would see it, too, Lora. But I was too pushy. I knew the Rainbow Bunch needed help. Money as well as manpower. I also knew they were looking for a fundraising chairperson. I thought Quinn might be interested."

"Sydney, I can't believe you ruined everything with Quinn because of this one incident!"

"Lora, he said he has no more challenges in his

life." Sydney spread her hands to explain. "Nothing to look forward to. I figured he's too young to do nothing but play retirement golf the rest of his life."

"That isn't for you to decide, Sydney. This is something Quinn must work out by himself. You can't direct his life. Or anyone's life, for that matter. Don't you know that by now?"

"You'd think I'd learn." Sydney heaved a sigh and moved to refill their coffee cups. "I got another call today from Mr. Thomas Francis, station manager of WFLA."

"You did?" Lora perked up. "The one who requested the film clip of you? What did he want?"

"A personal interview. Tomorrow, after work."

"Eeeee! That's great, Sydney!" Lora squealed excitedly.

Sydney smiled shyly. "He said they've reviewed the clip I sent and would like a personal interview. It's a good sign."

"Oh, Sydney, I'm so proud of you! This is one more step toward achieving your goal!" Lora grabbed her friend and hugged her happily. "How can you be so calm? Aren't you excited?"

"Yeah, sure. It's what I wanted, isn't it?" Sydney forced a smile. She only knew that the two weeks spent without Quinn had been absolutely miserable. Nothing, not even this job interview, had been able to lift her spirits.

"Then what's wrong?" Lora cast her friend a puzzled glance. "Oh, I see. This is something you want to discuss and share with Quinn."

"Not necessarily," Sydney fibbed. "I'd rather share it with someone who really cares. Like you, Lora. You

167

stood by me as a friend during all the rough times. I really appreciate it."

Lora took a seat across the table and shrugged. "Can I help it if I happen to think that Chad is the cutest kid since my own eighteen-year-old baby was five? I just didn't want to see him and his mom out on the streets. You've come a long way, Sydney!"

"I guess I have!" Sydney laughed and wrinkled her nose. "Remember the wine?"

Lora covered her eyes dramatically. "You discovered the hard way that wine has its own revenge!"

"You know something, Lora?" Sydney averred slowly. "This could be my ultimate revenge. If I get this job as sportscaster on WFLA, Daniel would surely have to see me! And he'd know I'm doing just fine without him. No, better than fine. He'd see I'm doing wonderfully without him! Oh, it would be my sweetest revenge!"

Lora watched Sydney warily. "Would it, Syd? Are you sure that's what you want?"

"Are you kidding? It's what I've always wanted!" Sydney's expression belied her tough words. "I do wish Quinn was around. But I can make it without Mr. Quinn Robinson, too. I can make it without anybody." In her heart, she knew she missed his arms around her more than anything in the world. And although she talked big, she wanted him even more than she wanted her sweet revenge.

Sydney spent the next day at work trying to look busy and stay calm. This interview at WFLA meant so much to her future. And it had happened so quickly, she could hardly believe it!

Keeping a lid on the exciting new job prospect was extremely difficult. She wanted to tell Dixie and Lee and *everyone!* And yet she didn't dare tell a soul at work. So she kept quiet and dodged everyone all day. In fact, she stayed so busy that she didn't even notice when Dixie spent an hour in Lee's office, then another hour with Lee and Mr. Reinhardt in the station manager's office.

What Sydney did observe was the resident sportscaster's routine. He didn't even show up at the station until after three. That meant he could sleep until noon. Not bad. Then he spent about an hour coordinating game scores with the corresponding tapes to be run, and another hour, it seemed, getting ready for the camera. What a nifty job!

Sydney rubbed her hands together and glanced in the mirror of the ladies' room. If she went on camera, she'd get a real hair stylist to do something wonderful with her hair. And she'd seek the advice of a professional makeup artist, one who coordinated her colors and facial shape to make her look her best under the lights. And of course, she'd have a manicurist do her nails. And—

Dixie poked her head in the door, interrupting Sydney's fancy daydreaming. "Oh, there you are! Lee wants to see you in his office."

"Now?" Sydney looked at her watch and grimaced. "It's after four. Can't it wait until tomorrow?" She was gearing up for this interview, and she didn't want to be distracted by some silly idea Lee had for a show.

"Yes, now! And no, it can't wait until tomorrow!" Dixie winked mischievously and disappeared.

Sydney sighed and trudged down the hall, taking

her own sweet time. Why now, only minutes from the biggest opportunity of my career? she thought. Lee means well, but he can be a total aggravation at times. He'll probably tell me about a couple who raises extinct bats. Or someone who sells bronzed buffalo chips and is making a fortune.

She poised her fist to knock on his office door, when she realized it was slightly ajar.

"Come on in, Sydney," Lee called, motioning to a chair when she entered. "Close the door. Have a seat. How about a Coke or something?" He reached into the compact refrigerator behind his chair. "I think I have a diet soda here. Want it?"

"Yes, thank you, Lee." She watched curiously. He had never offered her anything other than a scribbled sheet of paper filled with names, phone numbers, unusual hobbies or careers, and an order to "check this out." Today he was almost nice.

He handed over the soda. "Sydney, I'll get right to the point." He leaned his large arms on the desk. "Dixie's husband is being transferred to L.A. and, naturally, she'll be going with him. That means her job will be open. Now, I've already talked to Reinhardt about this and, since you're qualified and have the skills, we're prepared to offer you the job."

Sydney sat speechless for a moment, squeezing the canned drink. Was she dreaming? Or was he really offering her a job? How could this happen—today, of all days? "Community affairs director?" she managed to gasp.

He nodded. "Dixie recommended you highly, and I concur. She's agreed to give you some intensive training during the next two weeks before she leaves."

"Is that why she let me do so much by myself on the Rainbow Bunch production?"

"She's been threatening for some time that her husband would be transferred. She just didn't know when it would happen, so I asked her to keep quiet until we knew for sure. It gave us some time to think about replacing her. And to look around."

"Well, I don't know what to say, Lee. Of course I'm surprised."

He gestured magnanimously. "You'll have to discuss your salary with Reinhardt, Sydney. But believe me, it's going to be much better than you're making now. What do you think of that?" He leaned back and laced his fingers behind his head, obviously pleased with himself. He also expected her to jump at the wonderful opportunity he'd laid, gift-wrapped, at her feet.

"I'm sure the salary will be great. But, Lee, I need a little time to think about this." Sydney paused and licked her lips nervously. "It isn't that I'm not grateful for your confidence in me. I'm really flattered."

"What's to think about, Sydney?" Lee objected. "You'll be making more money. You'll be head of your own department, with lots of flexibility. Believe me, community affairs is not high priority with Reinhardt. You'll be free to shape it the way you want. There's a lot to be said for that. *I* don't have that kind of freedom. I have to answer for every move. Even this one."

"Oh, it sounds wonderful, Lee, but—"

He placed his palms down on the desk and leaned forward. "Okay, okay, take your time on this, Sydney. Sleep on it this weekend. We'll talk again Monday morning."

She blinked. In two days, she had to tell Lee her

answer. And if she didn't have one, what reason would she give? How could she delay it until she heard from WFLA? Was that really fair to Lee? But what about her needs? And what if—oh heavens, she needed help! Where was Quinn? She needed a friend. She needed Quinn.

When Sydney left Lee's office, she stopped by the ladies' room again. She slumped down at the little dressing table in front of the mirror. How could this be happening to her? Maybe she should just cancel this interview at WFLA and take Lee's offer. Maybe she should be honest with Lee and tell him she was seeking a job at a competitive station. But if she did that, would she be taking a chance on losing both jobs?

She straightened and looked in the mirror. A determined woman with profound green eyes and a resolute expression stared back. The smart businesswoman would leave all her options open and look honestly at both opportunities.

After running a quick brush through her tousled mass of auburn hair, Sydney rose. She had another interview to attend. Then, decision time.

At that moment, Dixie poked her head in the door again. "There you are, Sydney! I told you, Lee wanted to—"

"I talked to him, Dixie."

"And? What do you think?"

"Great, I guess."

"I think so, too. Oh, by the way, you had a phone message. Quinn called."

"Quinn?" Sydney fumbled the brush in her hand. So much for the smart businesswoman. "Is he on the line now?"

"No, he called a few minutes ago. You must have been talking with Lee. Well? You gonna take the job?"

"I . . . don't know yet. What did Quinn say?"

"Nothing." Dixie shrugged. "Just said to tell you he's back and he'll call later. You know, you're crazy if you don't take this, Sydney. I gotta go start packing. See you Monday."

Sydney stared blankly at the closed door. All she could think of was that Quinn had called. He was home and he wanted to talk to her and, oh dear God, she needed to talk to him! She'd go out to see him as soon as the interview was over. Lora was picking up Chad. Maybe she'd keep him a little longer. Sydney hugged her arms anxiously. She could hardly wait to see Quinn!

The interview at WFLA went well. So well, in fact, that they offered her the job immediately. Sportscaster. Sportscaster! This was *it!* Her sweet revenge!

The salary wasn't equal to her present one, but Mr. Francis assured her that it would improve once she came aboard. "We like to think of WFLA as one big happy family who'll welcome you with open arms, Sydney. Now, you couldn't expect to be a regular host right away. We want you to be on the weekend staff."

Well, she had to start somewhere, didn't she?

Sydney drove rapidly around Lakeshore Drive, anxious to tell Quinn her news. Two job offers! She couldn't wait to discuss her options with him. Couldn't wait to hold him, to feel his strong arms around her. Quinn would know what to do. He would give her sound advice.

She jerked the old Chevy to a halt in front of his house, and the first to greet her was Happy, the intrepid golden retriever. She petted him and laughed with delight as he jumped excitedly around her. Her euphoria must be contagious, even to the dog.

Trina opened the front door, and her young face broke into an instant grin. "Syd! I'm so glad you're here!"

"Hi, honey." Sydney opened her arms and Trina practically threw herself into them. "What a nice welcome! Are you okay, honey?"

"Oh, everything's happening this week. Mommy and Lindi and I are moving to Tallahassee! I'm so glad we'll be close to Daddy, but I hate to leave my friends in Lake City. Then in the middle of everything, my grampa got real sick. Everybody's all upset."

"I'm sorry about your grandfather, Trina. Is he in the hospital?"

The young girl nodded.

"Well, I'm sure he'll get better soon." Sydney hugged her again, and the two walked into the house arm in arm. "Where is your dad?"

"Out back." The girl gestured toward the patio. "We're having a picnic. I came in for the catsup when I heard you at the door. Come have a hamburger with us. There's plenty of food."

Sydney nodded and smiled assuredly, certain that there was enough food for an army and then some. Quinn always made sure of that. Trina reached for the catsup in the refrigerator, and Sydney caught a glimpse of the family gathered around the table. In the background, the pool sparkled with the last orange fingers of sunset.

She looked closer at the three figures. Her heart pounded with eager anticipation when she saw

Quinn's broad-shouldered back. And there was darling little Lindi, slipping Happy a french fry.

Across from them sat a woman. Stacey!

Dumbfounded, Sydney watched as Stacey reached across the table to clutch Quinn's hand! Her smiling, pretty face was aimed directly for Quinn's pleasure. And she was capturing his full attention.

Sydney saw purple! There was no way she would intrude on this cozy little family scene! She had to get out of there quickly! She wheeled around and gasped, "Trina, I must go. I forgot something important. Please, don't bother to tell Quinn I was here."

She dashed for her old Chevy and gunned it home. Chad was still across the hall at Lora's when she arrived, and she didn't even bother getting him. She couldn't deal with him right now. She could barely think straight.

Suddenly, she felt exhausted and just wanted to fall into bed and forget the world. But she couldn't stop the tears. And all the same old feelings she experienced when Daniel left came flooding back. Rejection, inadequacy, loneliness, anger!

It had happened again. Different man, different circumstances. But again she had been rejected by the man she loved.

It was all very clear. Stacey's father was extremely ill, and she and Quinn had drawn together in their time of sadness. And now she and the girls were moving in with him. Quinn would gather them close and take care of them all. How like him to generously take charge of a bad situation. It had all happened too fast for poor young Trina to understand. So Trina, in trying to grasp what was happening to her familiar life, had tried to bring Sydney into the tight little family circle.

However, Sydney knew that that circle didn't include her. She was once again out by herself. Just her and Chad. She threw herself onto the bed and cried. But this time there'd be no wine—she had learned a few lessons. She just hadn't learned how not to fall in love.

CHAPTER TWELVE

"Daddy, is Grampa going to die?"

Trina's young voice had a plaintive tone, and Quinn sat on the edge of her bed. He heaved a weary sigh. It had been a nerve-wracking week, but now his elderly former father-in-law was responding to treatment. They could all breathe easier. And Stacey felt safe to leave the hospital for a night's sleep, at his house, of course. "I don't think so, precious. He's been very sick, but the doctor believes he'll make it through this."

"Is that why Mommy's been so upset? And crying all the time?"

He brushed her blond curls back from her face. "Yes, Trina. You must understand that she's been worried and sad."

"But she told me that getting married would make her happy again," Trina said stubbornly.

"Well, that was before Grampa had this heart attack." Quinn smiled tightly in the darkness. Dear God, he hoped Stacey's marriage would make her happy. "I'm sure she'll feel much better after the marriage," he said with conviction.

"Can Lindi and I still come visit you? And sleep here?"

"Of course you can, precious. Things won't change around here. My home is for you and Lindi. You'll always be my little girls, and I will always have you with me, no matter what happens."

"Even if you marry Sydney, Daddy?"

"Marry Sydney?" Quinn gulped and managed to rasp, "Well, I don't know. Whatever made you think of that, precious?"

Trina yawned. "Well, with Mommy marrying Uncle Jack, I just thought you'd marry Sydney. I hope you do, 'cause she's lots of fun. Anyway, she promised to show me how to make a Dump Cake, whatever that is."

He laughed softly at the childish reasoning. "It's an easy, delicious cake, Trina. Great for Sunday mornings. Why don't we invite her out here this weekend so you two can make us a Dump Cake?"

"We could have done it tonight." Trina paused to yawn again. "But she forgot something and had to leave too soon."

Quinn stiffened. "Sydney was here? Tonight?"

"When we were eating supper. I told her we had plenty of food and invited her to stay, just like you always said to do. But she left anyway. She told me not to tell you, Daddy, and I thought it was because she wanted to surprise you. But she never came back to surprise you, did she?"

"No, precious, she didn't." Quinn frowned in the darkness. The last few days had been a hellish, crazy time during which he had made some major decisions about the direction of his life. After being out of town for three days, he'd returned to find Stacey at his house babbling about her pending marriage and that her father had had a heart attack. The girls were confused and upset. So Quinn had done what he could to appease them all. When Stacey's father showed some positive signs, she had rushed back to Quinn's home for solace.

Obviously, Sydney had seen Stacey on the patio and left immediately. She never could understand Stacey's presence, but maybe it was too much to expect of anyone.

"You'd better get to sleep, precious." He bent to kiss Trina's forehead. "Remember, I love you and Lindi with all my heart."

"Good night, Daddy. I love you, too."

Quinn shoved open the double doors and walked out onto the patio. He ran his hand raggedly around the back of his head. What a week it had been. Stacey continued to dominate everything in his life, and this week, in the face of crisis, she'd turned again to him. Of course Quinn cared about Stacey's father, but where was her future husband when she needed him? Uncle Jack, she'd called him for the kid's sake.

Damn! It took a child to point out the one woman who really counted to Quinn. The one he cared about over all others and who he wanted by his side. The one he'd deserted in his own frustration. *The one he loved.*

Quinn sighed heavily and walked around the pool. The water was dark and murky, for there was no moon tonight. No glittering stars, no reflections. But he could still see her face, hurt and puzzled, and he knew she'd fled from him and a strange situation that she would never understand. But then, maybe she shouldn't have to. Maybe it was time to let Stacey stand on her own. Time to turn his own life around. Time to go to Sydney and treat her like the very special person she was to him. And to love her. *Oh yes,* Quinn thought, *I do love you, Sydney!*

Quinn pounded impatiently on Sydney's apartment door. "Syd? Syd! Are you in there?" More pounding. "Syd! Open up!"

She flung open the door, looking red-eyed and disheveled, her eyes even greener than usual, her auburn hair more beautiful than he remembered. "Will you please shut up, Quinn? You'll have the manager calling me about all this racket in the hall!"

"Then let me in, because we have to talk."

She stepped back and shut the door behind him. Before she could turn around, he was speaking.

"I have only one thing to say. Sydney Jacques, I love you."

Sydney gasped and her hand flew to her head. Maybe she was dreaming. Two job offers and an "I love you" all in one day were just too much! She shook her head and turned away for a moment. When she looked back at him, Quinn was still there. Still handsome. And very serious.

She opened her mouth, but not a sound came out.

"Syd, are you all right?"

"I—I don't know, Quinn. It's too much. Too soon."

"I know this is sudden, but I can explain everything. I just realized that I want you very much." Without another word, he took her in his arms and kissed her thoroughly, taking her breath away, capturing her heart again. "Oh Syd, I love you so. I'm sorry about everything I've put you through. But I do love you."

Sydney looked up into the blue depths of his steady gaze. He was undeniably serious.

"Quinn, I tried to call and apologize, but you weren't home all week. I shouldn't have insisted you come watch the Rainbow Bunch. Or tried to entice you to work for them."

"Wrong." He smiled down at her. "That was one of the best things to ever happen to me."

"I don't understand."

"You are looking at the new fundraising chairman for the Rainbow Bunch. We're going national. Going to build a regional camp that can be used almost year round."

"But I thought you couldn't bear seeing those kids sick."

"I realized you were right. If everybody turned their heads, there'd be no one to help them. This is a real challenge, Syd!" He kissed her and swung her up in his arms.

"But—Stacey?"

"She's getting married. Someone named Jack. I'm taking back my key."

Relief and happiness flooded Sydney as she began to get the picture. "Trina said they were moving to Tallahassee. I thought they were moving in with you. Including Stacey. I love you, but man-sharing is not my style."

"I'll call her fiancé tomorrow and tell him to take her off my hands." Quinn paused and gave Sydney an apologetic grin. "Just a figure of speech, honey. From now on, it's going to be you and me, Syd."

181

"Sounds heavenly," she murmured as he nuzzled her neck.

"And Chad, of course." He kissed her nearest earlobe. "And Lindi and Trina, too."

"Heaven's getting crowded," she giggled.

Quinn headed for the bedroom. "And Happy."

"I knew it!" she groaned. "Quinn, this sounds serious if you're including the dog!"

He sat her on the bed. "I've never been more serious in my life. I'm going to make sure everything's perfect for you and me and our life together." He framed her face with his hands and began to kiss her fervently.

"Quinn, please," she murmured, forcing them apart. "I don't think I can continue like this with no strings attached."

"Oh, my Sydney, I want strings. And rings. And all the things that go with a family. I want to pamper you. And give you things. And take you places. And make you happy. And love you."

"Quinn, I love you, but I'm afraid I need a commitment." Her green eyes were troubled. Would her needs scare him away?

"And I'll admit I want to possess you, Sydney, with marriage. I love you with all my heart. And I'll never leave you."

"Promise?" she whispered breathlessly.

"Never!" His lips claimed hers with such strong conviction, there was no doubt about his pledge. It was a commitment of love she had to believe. He embraced her tenderly, his kisses covering her face until she melted against him and returned his kisses with equal fervor.

They made love slowly, ardently, and with adulation, each committing to the other, each possessing the other. Gently ambling streams of desire meandered through their veins and souls, gradually growing in strength and velocity. Quiet rivulets became coursing currents that grew to bubbling hot springs of love, welling up to overflowing.

They exchanged private vows of love as the fiery flow became a hot volcano of passion, rushing, mingling, merging into a torrent of possession—and commitment—and love.

Later, they called Lora and asked if Chad could spend the night. She agreed readily. No explanation was necessary. Still later, they foraged in the kitchen for a late-night omelet and a small glass of wine to toast their engagement.

"Tomorrow we'll get an appropriate ring, maybe a ruby surrounded with diamonds." Quinn kissed the knuckles of her left hand and pulled her down onto the sofa with him. "Then we'll go home and—"

"Throw Stacey out!" Sydney laughed.

"Yes." He grinned at her wickedness. "And there is a little girl who is waiting for you to teach her how to make a Dump Cake."

"I'd like nothing better than to start our own Sunday-morning family tradition," Sydney said.

"Nothing?"

"Well, *almost* nothing." She smiled and fed him a bite of cheese omelet. "I can't believe today really happened. Two job offers and one proposal in one day. For me, that's impossible!"

He scratched his chin. "I think I know the answer to the proposal. But what about the job offers?"

"One is for weekend sportscaster for WFLA. And

the other is to replace my boss as community affairs director at WTAL."

"Which one do you really want, Syd?"

"That's why I came out to see you earlier. I needed your advice." She took a slow sip of wine. "The sportscaster job is one I've always wanted. But I must admit, I've really enjoyed the community affairs department. I'd have some latitude to develop it my own way."

Quinn nodded. "What'll it be? A new challenge for your future, or revenge for something in the past?"

She nestled in the strong shelter of his arm. "Working weekends at WFLA sounds like a real bummer. I think I'd love developing the community affairs department. You know something, Quinn? I don't need my sweet revenge any more. I have you."

"We have each other, honey. And love." He pulled her into his lap. "What more do we need?"

Between kisses she giggled. "Well, there's Chad and Lindi and Trina . . ."

"And Happy!"

"Yes, I'm very happy!" Sydney smiled and returned his kiss, knowing deep in her heart that this was just the beginning of a joyful life with Quinn.

EPILOGUE

Two months later, the family gathered in the living room of the beautiful contemporary house on Lakeshore Drive. Lindi, who now challenged Chad like any little sister would her brother, raced through the house and beat him to the beanbag chair. Grumbling, he grabbed a huge pillow and straddled it, cowboy style. Trina, who would soon be eight and too old to associate with the two little ones, sat sedately on a side chair by herself. And Happy, who had never been more content now that he had a rowdy little boy to romp with, curled up near the door.

"And now we present," Quinn announced loudly as he slipped the cassette into the VCR, "summer camp with the Rainbow Bunch, plus a special appearance by the amazing gymnast, Sydney Robinson!"

Everyone shrieked with laughter, for they knew what was coming.

"And as an added attraction on the same tape," Quinn continued in his ringmaster's voice, "the wedding of the amazing gymnast and the magnificent hero of the day!"

More laughter from the kids.

Sydney gave her husband an indulgent smile.

185

"You're lucky that tolerance is one of my virtues, Mr. Robinson."

"I certainly hope so." He joined her on the sofa. "Because we have a lifetime to review this tape with our kids and our grandkids and our—"

"Please!" she moaned. "I'm still adjusting to my new family of five! Six, counting Happy."

There were appropriate comments and warm chuckles as the kids watched and recalled each special event recorded on tape. They had all spent a very rewarding week at the newly purchased camp with the Rainbow Bunch at the end of August. Even Chad, Lindi, and Trina acted as junior counselors.

"Here she comes!" shrieked Lindi.

They all watched the screen in rapt attention as Sydney guided a canoe up to the dock. The two children in the front of the canoe stood up and instantly, as if on cue, Sydney flipped overboard!

Everyone howled with laughter.

"You can see it wasn't my fault!" Sydney protested loudly. "Nobody bothered to tell those kids not to stand in a canoe."

"The amazing gymnast, my mom!" laughed Chad.

"Some things never change," Quinn said, giving her a chaste kiss on the cheek.

She smiled up into his adoring blue eyes. "Like our love?"

"Yes."

"Look!" Trina uttered with a certain reverence. "Here comes the bride!"

They turned back to the screen as Sydney, looking absolutely beautiful in a pale yellow dress with flowers

186

in her hair, joined hands with Quinn beneath the pines at the campground.

"I don't know how anyone could ever have a prettier wedding," Sydney claimed. "Nor prettier flower children!"

"At least you didn't fall in the lake again, Mom!"

"That's because we weren't standing near it," Quinn responded.

Sydney grabbed a pillow and pounded him with it until Quinn defended himself by discarding the pillow and grasping her in a bear hug and kissing her until she yelled uncle. Then the kids all laughed and teased as he pressed his lips to hers in a long, lasting kiss.

"Take that, Mrs. Robinson. Forever."

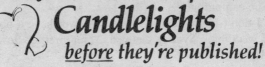

LAURA LONDON

Let her magical romances enchant you with their tenderness.

For glorious storytelling at its very best, get lost in these Regency romances.

___ A HEART TOO PROUD	13498-6	$2.95
___ THE BAD BARON'S DAUGHTER	10735-0	2.95
___ THE GYPSY HEIRESS	12960-5	2.95
___ LOVE'S A STAGE	15387-5	2.95
___ MOONLIGHT MIST	15464-4	2.95